hot
cocoa
hearts

Also by Suzanne Nelson

Cake Pop Crush

Macarons at Midnight

You're Bacon Me Crazy

Serendipity's Footsteps

hot
cocoa
hearts

Suzanne Nelson

SCHOLASTIC INC.

Copyright © 2015 by Suzanne Nelson

All rights reserved. Published by Scholastic Inc., *Publishers since 1920*. SCHOLASTIC and associated logos are trademarks and/or registered trademarks of Scholastic Inc.

The publisher does not have any control over and does not assume any responsibility for author or third-party websites or their content.

No part of this publication may be reproduced, stored in a retrieval system, or transmitted in any form or by any means, electronic, mechanical, photocopying, recording, or otherwise, without written permission of the publisher. For information regarding permission, write to Scholastic Inc., Attention: Permissions Department, 557 Broadway, New York, NY 10012.

This book is a work of fiction. Names, characters, places, and incidents are either the product of the author's imagination or are used fictitiously, and any resemblance to actual persons, living or dead, business establishments, events, or locales is entirely coincidental.

ISBN 978-0-545-92889-2

10 9 8 7 6 5 4 3 2 1   16 17 18 19 20

Printed in the U.S.A.   40
First printing 2016

Book design by Jennifer Rinaldi and Yaffa Jaskoll

In memory of Liz Teed, inspiring teacher and one of the first fans of Cake Pop Crush and its offspring.

You are missed.

—S.N.

Chapter One

"I'm not coming out. *Ever.*"

I curled up my legs, blinding in their green-and-white-striped tights. Then I scooted farther back into the plastic child-sized gingerbread cottage. I'd made up my mind. I was going to stay here until: (1) My parents gave in or (2) I turned eighteen and didn't have to listen to them anymore.

A red-cheeked Santa ducked his head through the tiny window.

"Ho, ho, ho!" he bellowed. "What's this I hear about a certain elf going on strike?" He winked. "Don't you want to bring joy to lots of little girls and boys this Christmas, Emery Elf?"

I rolled my eyes, giving my cherry-red romper a resentful tug. This crimson monstrosity, brighter and tackier than Rudolph's nose, had replaced my favorite *Dark Side of the Moon* tee, my purple plaid skirt, and black leggings.

"Dad, would you please quit the Santa act already?" I groaned.

"Break character? Never." His blue eyes twinkled with annoying cheer.

I grimaced. "I'm protesting Christmas." I motioned to the walls of the cottage. "I'm staging a sit-in."

There was a pounding on the roof, which was only an inch above my head. "Emery Mason." Mom's stern voice hissed from outside. "This is the price you have to pay for breaking curfew."

"But that was for the sake of my art!" I objected. "You of all people should get that!" I was hoping to appeal to her creative side—the one that made her chronically burn casseroles and lose car keys in favor of snapping pictures. If anyone could understand forgetting yourself in the moment, it was Mom.

My plan didn't work.

"You come out right now and do your job," she said, "or you'll be staging a sit-in in your room. *Permanently.*"

Sure, I'd broken my curfew last Friday night. But how could my parents blame me? The moon and stars had been so bright, and the air had that crackling winter coldness to it—perfect for photography. I'd been at the park, trying to get a mood shot of the moon through a bramble of bare tree branches. I'd planned to be back home by nine, but I forgot to bring my cell, so I couldn't set my phone alarm as a reminder. Before I knew it, curfew came and went.

Now Mom and Dad were making me pay for it. Big-time. It was bad enough that every year, my parents became Mr. and Mrs. Claus incarnate, bubbling over with ridiculous amounts of holiday cheer. Now they'd dragged me into it, forcing me to work for them for the whole month of December—the busiest time for their portrait studio business. To make matters worse, they were running a Santa photo booth at the Fairview Mall, and yours truly was being put to work as Emery the Helpful Elf.

I sighed, stuck on my plastic pointed elf ears, and stood up, instantly banging my head against the roof. Then I crawled out the candy-cane-striped door and into the Nightmare Before Christmas.

The North Pole Wonderland photo booth hadn't even opened yet, but already, there were two dozen kids and their parents lined up for pictures with Santa (aka Dad in his beloved Santa suit). The Fairview Mall was crammed with bustling Saturday crowds eager for holiday shopping sprees. A manic, head-splitting version of "Jingle Bells" was blaring through the main concourse. Giant ornaments and snowflakes hung from sky-lights overhead, and twinkling garland draped across every inch of the second-floor railings. There was even an entire store called Holiday Heaven, stocked with every Christmas trinket, snow globe, or centerpiece known to mankind. And—even more ludicrous—the store was using half a dozen live penguins in its window display! The mall had gone Christmas crazy.

"Look, Mommy!" a child in line shrieked. "It's one of Santa's elves."

Dad nudged me as he headed through the mountains of artificial snow toward his sleigh. "That's your cue," he whispered.

Oh joy. I raised my hand in a weak wave just as Mom breezed by me.

"Em," she said, "have you seen my camera bag?" She paused to take in my outfit. "And do you have to wear those black boots? Didn't the costume come with pointy slippers?"

I shrugged. "Couldn't find them," I lied. In reality, my elf slippers were buried in the back of my closet. "Besides, I'm *not* giving up my Doc Martens. Aren't the elf ears humiliating enough?"

I was praying that none of my other friends would see me in this getup, especially Sawyer Kade. He was the unspoken leader of the Undergrounds, the group I hung with at school. He was also the lead singer of Sweet Garbage, a band he'd started out of his garage. Just thinking about Sawyer was enough to set my heart racing. An image of him flashed before my eyes—his messy, purple-tipped hair and amber eyes, and that moody, quiet air he gave off when he was deep in thought over his lyrics.

I'm not sure Sawyer and I qualified as friends, since he'd never actually spoken to me before. We may have been a part of the same friend group, but there are so many of us in the Undergrounds that the two of us had never officially crossed paths. Still, I'd had a crush on him since, well, forever.

Mom waved her hand at me distractedly as she glanced around for her bag. "Okay, okay. Wear the boots." She kissed my forehead, then gave the bell on my elf hat a playful tug. "But work on the attitude, please. You're going to have a good time. You'll see."

"Maybe I would, if you let me take the pictures."

"Em, we talked about this." She puffed her cheeks in exasperation as she adjusted her lighting equipment. "Parents want their kids' photos with Santa to be more . . ." She paused, searching for the right word. "Traditional."

"Oh, I get it." I kicked at an unsuspecting Styrofoam gingerbread man in the snow, knocking him over. "My photos are too weird for holiday cards, right?"

"I didn't say that." Her eyes met mine with a "let's not do this" look. "You know I love your style. But it's not the right fit for this type of thing." She bent to fix the fallen gingerbread man, then straightened as the blaring music suddenly stopped and a voice came over the loudspeaker.

"Attention, holiday shoppers," it boomed. "This is an

important security announcement. A penguin has escaped from the Holiday Heaven window display. It was last spotted headed for the fountain on the main promenade. Please report any sightings to the Welcome Kiosk as soon as possible. Do not attempt to apprehend the animal alone. Thank you."

"See?" I said. "Even the penguins want to escape."

Mom glared at me. "Funny. Now, can we get ready to start greeting our customers? Please?"

"Fine." I sighed. "And by the way, your camera bag is hanging around Blitzen's neck." I nodded toward the nine plastic reindeer harnessed to Santa's sleigh.

Relief swept Mom's face. "Thanks, sweetie." She slid her camera out of the bag, checked to see that Dad was ready in his sleigh, then smiled at me. "Okay. Let them in."

I walked over to the front of the line, took the first photo order package from an eager mom, and unlatched the gate to the North Pole Wonderland.

"Hi there, boys and girls!" I called out to the droves of kids. I struggled for an enthusiasm I didn't feel. "Who wants to sit on Santa's lap?"

On cue, the boy at the front of the line stomped on my foot, the two behind him started whacking each other with candy canes, and a toddler in a red velvet dress burst into tears. The melody from my least favorite carol popped into my head: *On the first day of Christmas, my parents gave to me, some kids screaming miserab-ly.*

And the day was just beginning.

Three hours later, I had gone from grumpy to downright Grinchy. If the tears from kids and the frowns from their parents were any indication, the photo booth was an absolute disaster. Most of the kids were more interested in pulling off my dad's Santa beard than in sitting still for a photo, and those who did sit still were frozen with fear. The line had gotten even longer over the course of the morning, I could hear people grumbling about being hungry for lunch, and even Mom and Dad's cheer was waning.

"How much longer, miss?" a mother called from somewhere in the crowd. "We've been waiting for over an hour!"

"We're working as quickly as we can," I offered, trying hard not say it through clenched teeth. I took a pale-faced little boy by the hand. Poor kid. He probably wanted to spend the day sledding, and here he was, stuffed into a suit jacket and tie for the perfect Kodak moment.

"Are you ready to get your picture taken with Santa?" I asked, hoping to get a smile out of him. His lip started quivering. Not a good sign. All it took was one glance at my dad in the sleigh for him to start bawling.

"Stop that, Tommy!" his mom scolded. "Just lift him up there," she insisted. "He'll calm down in a second."

I hesitated but remembered my parents' mantra: The customer is always right.

"Okay," I said. I placed my hands around Tommy's chest, ready to hoist him into the sleigh, when suddenly . . .

"Yow!" I yanked back, clutching my right hand. "He bit me!"

"No," his mom said. "He would never do that."

"But—but—" I stammered in shock and fury while my dad gushed apologies, shooting me a warning look not to lose my temper.

Tommy grinned triumphantly and ran into the gingerbread house to hide while his mom turned back to me. "If you can't do your job," she snapped, "I want my money back."

"Fine." I handed her back her order form as I seethed, ready to tell her exactly what I *really* thought. I mean, what were Mom and Dad going to do, fire me? I wish! "You know what?" I started. "Your son is—"

"Hungry!" a voice behind me announced.

Huh? I spun around to see a dark-haired boy my age holding a tray filled with cookies and small red cups brimming with marshmallows. He wore a sweater almost as tacky as my elf outfit: It was green-and-red-striped and had a gargantuan Rudolph with a blinking red nose plastered across its front.

"Who would like to try Santa's Magic Hot Chocolate?" the guy asked, and was met with kids' cheers and parents' resounding applause. "I think Tommy should get the first one," he said, loud enough so Tommy could surely hear, even inside the gingerbread house. "Too bad we can't find him anywhere."

That was all it took for Tommy to come bursting out of the house, all smiles.

"Thank goodness he came," my dad mumbled to me as he climbed down from the sleigh.

"Who is he?" I asked.

"Alejandro Perez," my dad said. "His grandfather owns Cocoa Cravings, the hot chocolate shop over there." Dad nodded toward a store only a few steps across the concourse from the North Pole Wonderland. Inside, a white-haired older man I guessed was Alejandro's grandfather was standing behind the counter. "We agreed to let them hand out hot chocolate samples to people in line to help promote their business. And I don't think it's going to hurt ours any, either."

I watched Alejandro as he wove through the line, handing out cups and making easy conversation with the customers.

"You know," he said, bending toward one little girl conspiratorially, "Santa always drinks this on Christmas Eve, right before he delivers presents. It's made fresh up at the North Pole." The girl giggled as Alejandro winked. His thick black curls hugged his forehead, and he was so cheerful that even his glinting dark eyes seemed to be smiling. He was definitely giving off that wide-eyed, boy-next-door vibe. I might've even thought he had a kind of naïve cuteness if I'd been in a better mood. But right now, all I could do was stare, wondering how he could maintain that sappy expression amidst hordes of tantruming kids. It had to be an act.

But his mood seemed to be contagious, because within seconds of taking sips of their hot chocolate, customers relaxed into happiness. Even Tommy was sitting in the sleigh unprompted now, waiting patiently for Dad to join him.

"Wow," I muttered in disbelief. "What's in that hot chocolate?"

Alejandro must've heard me, because he walked over, giving me a wave. "Hey, Emery, how's it going?"

"Hey," I said, taken aback that he was acting like he knew me, when I couldn't remember ever having seen him before. "Alejandro, right?"

"Alex for short." He was still smiling. Did he ever stop? He tilted his head inquisitively, as if he knew I was drawing a blank on him. "You don't recognize me, do you?"

"No," I mumbled, blushing in spite of myself. "Sorry."

He shrugged, laughing. "I'm in eighth grade with you at

Fairview. I just moved here from California last month. I'm staying with Abuelo, my grandpa, until my parents wrap up their jobs in San Diego. They wanted me to come here ahead of them so I wouldn't miss the beginning of next semester." He handed out a few more steaming cups. "I'm not that surprised you haven't seen me at school. We don't really move in the same circles."

I saw how this could be true. My friends and I prided ourselves on moving against the tide, spending our lunch periods discussing art and music instead of the latest gossip. Above all, we didn't believe in faking anything, especially emotion. And I had a feeling that Alex here was a seasoned pro at the on-demand smile, legit or not.

Alex held a cup out to me. "Here. Try some. You look like you could use it."

"Thanks," I said, waving the cup away, "but I don't like hot chocolate."

"Who ever heard of an elf that doesn't like hot chocolate?" He laughed. "Isn't that against the big guy's rules?" There was a teasing glimmer in his eyes.

"It's not my thing. Too sweet and syrupy. Ick." I shook my head, grimacing.

His eyes widened. "Man, if you've got something against hot chocolate, you must be having one *bad* day."

"*Bad* is an understatement." We stepped back as Mom moved in with her camera to snap the photos of Tommy with Dad. I popped a piece of my favorite hard candy, Venom, into my mouth. The tart watermelon and spicy pepper flavors zinged over my taste buds, cheering me up a bit. Then, while Alex handed out the rest of the hot chocolates, I recounted every detail of my traumatic morning to him. It felt so good to unload all of my frustrations, even onto a stranger. "I've been bitten, stomped on, and yelled at," I finished in summary, "and if I hear one more Christmas song, I'll scream." I sighed. "I hate the holiday season."

Alex laughed. "You hate Christmas? I love this time of year!"

"Somehow, that doesn't surprise me." I motioned to his sweater.

"Hey, if you can't wear an ugly sweater at Christmastime, when can you? Besides, it's my work uniform. Abuelo has Frosty the Snowman on his."

I couldn't help grinning at that.

"So, what's your problem with Christmas?" He leaned closer, whispering, "Wait, don't tell me. Your grandpa got run over by a reindeer?"

I laughed. It was impossible not to. He was funny, I had to give him that. "Christmas," I said, "is a completely commercialized holiday that feeds on materialism. It's just another way for stores to make money off customers who feel obligated to buy meaningless gifts for people they probably don't even like."

"Whoa." Alex shook his head, holding up a hand for mercy. "I wonder if they offer elf training workshops in anger management."

I wanted to look mad, but another laugh broke through instead.

"Seriously, though," he said, his eyes holding mine. "It's too bad you feel that way. Christmas is the season of love and giving . . ."

As if on cue, a child's voice rose up from the line, whining, "But *why* won't you buy me that doll, Mommy? It's only thirty dollars, and you said I could have a treat today!"

I jerked my thumb in the direction of the voice. "See? Nothing but 'gimme gimme.'"

Alex only smiled. "You can't blame an overtired kid for trying." He shrugged. "And if you're hoping to convert me, it's not going to work."

I raised a skeptical eyebrow at him. "There's no way you can stay legitimately happy through all of this."

"So what are you saying? That I'm faking it?" He studied me in a thoughtful way that made me fidget self-consciously with my costume. It was like his eyes were searching for something inside of me I didn't even know was there. It was unsettling, *and* irritating.

"Yeah," I admitted. "Maybe you are."

"Or . . ." He leaned toward me, jingling the bell on my hat, and warmth flooded through me. I felt momentarily disoriented at his closeness. "Maybe you're wrong. And maybe *I* can change your mind. Starting with hot chocolate."

I snorted, the spell broken. "I don't change my mind about much. Just ask my parents."

"Then you're in even worse shape than I thought." He shook

his head at me, then looked past me toward Cocoa Cravings, where his *abuelo* was motioning him over. "I've got to get back to the shop." He picked up his empty tray. "But since we're going to be working next door to each other, I'm sure I'll see you again. Better watch out. Optimism can be contagious, you know."

I rolled my eyes. "I'm immune."

He turned to walk away, but as he did, a small penguin waddled in front of him, followed by two puffing, out-of-shape security guards.

"Come back here, Happy Feet!" one of them hollered.

Alex and I looked at each other, then burst out laughing.

He started walking again, calling over his shoulder, "See you around, Scrooge!"

I stared after him, surprised by how much I had laughed today.

"Break time's over," Mom said, tapping me on the shoulder. "I need you to help set up the next shot." When I hesitated, Mom handed me a basket of candy canes. "Well, come on, Em! Get over there and spread some cheer."

I sighed. This was going to be the longest holiday season of my life.

Chapter Two

"There should be a law against this," I said, staring at the front of Fairview Middle School. Giant paper snowflakes were plastered on the walls, with twinkly lights surrounding them. A human-sized inflatable snowman greeted me as I walked in. I felt like I was in a winter wonder-nightmare.

I grimaced at my best friend, Jez, who was trying to give me a sympathetic look through her giggles. I'd spent our walk to school filling her in on my traumatic experience at the North Pole Wonderland. "And to think I was actually looking forward to school today. I figured it couldn't possibly be worse than all that deck-the-malls madness."

Jez tugged one of my teased-out pigtails, a sign of BFF affection she'd been giving me since elementary school. "Oh, that reminds me!" she exclaimed. "I wrote you a consolation poem." Jez loved to write haiku, and they usually involved stuff like flightless sparrows or barren wastelands. They were good, even if they were depressing. Now she flipped open her notepad and read, "Minimum-wage elf, candy canes stuck in your hair, next year . . . Hanukkah?"

"Hilarious." I gave her a good-natured eye roll.

"What can I say? I try." She fluffed the crinoline on her lime-green tutu. Tutus were Jez's signature article of clothing, and her way of rebelling against her very traditional Indian parents, who made her wear a sari at every family get-together she had to attend. "Come on." She took my arm and led me into the main hallway.

Miniature wreaths and blue-and-white menorahs hung from the ceiling. It wasn't as bad as the mall, at least.

"Good morning, ladies!" Principal Michaels greeted us as he

passed our lockers. "Be sure to check out the cafeteria's hot lunch! Holiday-themed this whole month. Today's special is mistletoe meat loaf with Yule-log yams."

I shook my head shut and clenched my eyes. "Please. I can't take anymore."

"Sorry, Em," Jez said with a laugh as she steered me to my homeroom door. Then I felt her elbow me.

I opened my eyes. There was Sawyer, walking toward the classroom with that brooding lope of his, head low, headphones on, like he was puzzling over the world's greatest mysteries and he wasn't about to let something as ordinary as school get in the way. He exuded the sort of easy nonchalance that made teachers nervous, and made me weak in the knees.

I held my breath as he neared. Maybe today would be the day. Today, he'd glance up, our eyes would meet, and there'd be the zing of an instant connection between us. He'd wonder how he'd never noticed me before, and without even needing to speak, we'd both realize how perfect we were for each other. He'd lean toward me . . .

"Emery!" Jez's voice broke through my daydream just as the

bell rang. I blinked and saw that the hallway had nearly emptied out. Sawyer had breezed right by me into the classroom without even a nod. "I've got to go," Jez said with a mischievous grin. "Have fun Sawyer gazing. See you in gym!"

"Yeah, yeah," I mumbled. The fact of the matter was Sawyer was about as untouchable as a star, and gazing was all I'd ever had the courage to do.

I sat down at my desk just as Mrs. Finnegan walked in wearing a flame-red sweater with kissing polar bears on it and earrings in the shape of tree ornaments. Criminy. I should've guessed Mrs. Finnegan would go all out for Christmas. She was the sort of person who wore themed sweaters for every season—not just the holidays.

"Season's greetings, ladies and gentlemen," she said as soon as the morning announcements were finished. "Now that the holidays are approaching, I thought we could all participate in a fun project to get into the spirit of giving." She clapped her hands enthusiastically, and expectant whispers flew around the room. "That's right," she singsonged. "It's Secret Santa time!"

"Ooh, I love Secret Santa!" Nyssa Vanderfeld cried, giving a thrilled golf clap. "We do it every year at Daddy's country club party, and last year I got a Coach clutch."

"How . . . generous," Mrs. Finnegan said politely, and I almost laughed. Nyssa was the prissiest girl in our homeroom, but because she had an amazing voice that had won the glee club every competition it had entered, she had a slew of admirers, including some of the faculty. Rumor had it that her dad, a music-industry mogul, was trying to land her a recording contract. She lived in a mansion-adorned part of town called Hillcrest Abbey.

Mrs. Finnegan, though, never seemed starry-eyed around Nyssa, and now she cleared her throat as she surveyed the rest of the class. "For *our* Secret Santa, the maximum amount you may spend on gifts is thirty dollars."

"Oh." Nyssa's tone drooped in disappointment. "Well, will the whole eighth grade be participating?" she asked. I guessed she was hoping she might pull the name of one of her many crushes who was in some other class.

"This is just for our homeroom," Mrs. Finnegan said.

Nyssa's lips pursed, and she gave a sigh. Her attitude wasn't surprising. Nyssa seemed to have a superiority complex that could rival any royal's.

I slumped down in my chair, my mood instantly darkening. This was exactly why I hated this sort of thing. Why couldn't teachers accept that walls built by cliques couldn't be torn down with cheesy, forced gift giving?

"There are four weeks until winter break," Mrs. Finnegan went on, "and you'll give your Secret Santa one gift each week. Each week will have a different theme." She turned to the Smart Board at the front of the classroom, and wrote a list:

Week 1: The Gift of Food
Week 2: The Gift of Fun
Week 3: The Gift of Craft
Week 4: The Gift of Heart

"The themes are fairly self-explanatory," she continued, "but in case you need clarification, week one can be a tasty treat—it doesn't have to be homemade, unless you like to bake. Week two can be a gag gift. In good taste, of course." She raised an eyebrow at Vince Gould, the class prankster, and he gave her an innocent "who me?" look back. "Week three should be something handmade, and week four will be the biggest gift, which will be exchanged during our holiday party on December twenty first, the Friday before winter break."

Then Mrs. Finnegan pulled a Santa hat out from under her desk and began walking down the rows with it, letting students reach in to pull out a name. Everyone around me was twittering excitedly, giggling like kids half their age. Except for Sawyer. He was watching the Santa hat circle the room with an expression of impassive amusement on his face.

My heart warmed with a feeling of kinship, and then a thought struck me. What if I pulled his name out of the hat and became his Secret Santa? As unenthused as I was by the idea of Secret Santas, my heart still sped up at the idea of getting Sawyer. If that happened, I could finally show him just how well I understood him, and how perfect we were for each other.

"Now, remember, the name you get should be kept an absolute secret. No spoiling the surprise," Mrs. Finnegan was saying. She stopped next to my desk and held the Santa hat out to me, smiling encouragingly. I reached in, a vision of Sawyer's name dancing in my head. But when I read the name on the slip of paper in my hand, my heart sank: Nyssa. Of all the people, I'd gotten stuck with her.

I sighed, wondering how I was ever going to think up gift ideas for a girl who had everything. Then I watched as Sawyer pulled a paper from the hat. A furtive smile crossed his face as he read the mystery name, and I felt a pang of jealousy toward whichever lucky person could bring something so rare to the surface. Sawyer's smiles were fleeting and few.

"All right," Mrs. Finnegan said when the hat was emptied of names, "your first gift should be delivered by this Friday. It doesn't have to be given during class. The time and place are up to you."

Great. How about nowhere, and never?

"The whole world is conspiring against me," I grumbled to Jez on our walk home from school. "I mean, look at this place." I motioned to the lights and garland strung around every lamppost on Main Street. "I Saw Mommy Kissing Santa Claus" was blasting from speakers mounted on the roof of the town hall, and there were carolers dressed in Victorian costumes singing along on the front steps, way too merrily. In the hours I'd spent at school, Fairview had transformed itself. It may have been a small New Jersey town, but what it lacked in size, it made up for in spirit. It never skimped on Christmas.

"Come on, Em. It's no different from every other year," Jez said.

"I don't remember seeing *them* last year, do you?" I jerked my head toward the town hall, where a trio of people dressed in overstuffed snowmen costumes were jingling sleigh bells and handing out flyers.

Jez gave them a side glance and giggled. "Uh-oh. They're headed straight for us."

"Omigod. Walk faster," I whispered. Too late.

The tallest snowman jabbed a flyer right in my face.

"No, thanks," I muttered, ducking my head into my coat. In the glimpse I'd gotten of the flyer, I'd seen that it was advertising Fairview's Holiday Stroll. On the Saturday before Christmas, hundreds of folks descended into the town square for the annual tradition. People "strolled" through the streets, drinking hot chocolate and oohing and aahing at decorated houses and ice sculptures.

"I'll take one!" Jez said cheerily.

"Hey! You don't even celebrate Christmas!" I pointed out.

"So? That doesn't mean I can't appreciate it." She smiled, casting her gaze up and down Main Street. "The lights, the music. It's all so cheery."

I shook my head. "My best friend. A wannabe Cindy-Lou Who."

Jez shrugged as she turned onto Millstone Lane toward her house. "Talk to you later!" she called over her shoulder.

I waved back and then walked the two short blocks to Willow Court, my street. The second I spotted my house, I stopped dead, staring.

It was true, I should've been expecting it. It happened around this time every year. But still, the eight-foot inflatable snow globe looming in the middle of our front yard seemed even more garish than I remembered. A few feet from the snow globe sat Santa's workshop, a plywood cottage Dad had built complete with an animatronic Santa building toys inside. And the whole yard was littered with storage bags and enormous boxes over-flowing with light-up reindeer, singing polar bears, glittery plastic penguins—every Christmas decoration in the universe.

My dad was balanced precariously on a ladder leaning against one of our house's three gables. Only his head was visible above the tangled mass of blinking colored lights he was holding.

"Hi, honey!" He smiled at me as he climbed down the ladder. "Guess what I'm working on this afternoon?"

"The Holly Jolly House," I mumbled.

"You got it!" my dad said with a snap of his fingers.

The Holly Jolly House was Dad's name for the sprawling dis-play that he and my mom set up in our yard every Christmas. It grew each year as my dad constructed more elaborate backdrops and choreographed more complicated movements for all of the animated parts. In truth, the Holly Jolly House could've outdone any ride at Disney World, and it had achieved a surprising amount of fame in Fairview. Our house was in the historic dis-trict in town, and with all its eves and gables, it was an ideal house to dress up with thousands of lights and decorations.

People stood in line for hours during the Holiday Stroll for a chance to walk past our house in all its yuletide glory.

Dad dug through one of the boxes and pulled out a three-foot plastic mouse peeking out of a stocking. "What do you think? Should I put Hector on the front porch this time? Last year I think he felt left out of the action, stuck over by the hydrangea bush."

"Um, sure," I said flatly, wanting to sink into the ground and disappear. My dad also had this completely mortifying habit of naming every creature that was stirring in his Holly Jolly House, and he was always ready with assessments on their emotional well-being, too.

Now he wiped sweat from his brow. "This old Kriss Kringle could really use your help. My back's not what it used to be. How about you trade in your book bag for a hammer, hon? It'll be like old times."

I hesitated, looking into his expectant face. There had been a time, years ago, when I'd been so excited about setting up the Holly Jolly House that I begged for it as early as Halloween. But

I wasn't little anymore, and where I'd once seen magic in the lights and music, now I saw fading, cracked plastic and cheap lawn ornaments.

"Actually, Dad, I have a lot of homework." I stared at the ground. "I was really hoping to get some time in with my camera later, too . . ."

"Sure, sure," Dad said in a quieter voice, "homework comes first, of course. No problem." He turned back to the box full of decorations. "Better go in and get started on it. We can catch up at dinner."

"Okay," I said with a mixture of relief and guilt. I hated disappointing him, but didn't he see that I wasn't a gullible little kid anymore? As I walked past him to the front porch, I caught a glimpse of Mom watching us from her studio window.

When I opened the door, she was waiting for me in the foyer, messy papers clutched in her arms. "Hey there," she said, "you haven't seen a pile of invoices lying around, have you? I promised your dad I'd find them so he can finish up this month's accounting for the business. I thought I had them in a red folder . . . somewhere . . ." She scuttled past me into the family room to thumb through another of the perpetual piles of paperwork that sprang up all over our house.

"Haven't seen them," I said. "Sorry." I tried to avoid her eyes, but she paused midsearch, giving me a scrutinizing look.

"What happened outside just now?" she asked. "Your dad told me he was hoping you'd help with the decorating. Now he looks like someone who's just been told there's no such thing as Santa."

"*Mom*," I said, incensed, "there *is* no such thing as Santa."

"Careful." She wagged a finger at me. "You don't want to be on the naughty list."

"Argh! Don't you start, too!" I threw up my arms. "I have homework, so I took a rain check on the decorating. That's all."

"Oh, Emery." Mom didn't have to say aloud that she was disappointed in me. Her soft, sagging tone said it all. "The Holly Jolly House means so much to your dad. When he was growing up, there were so many years when his family couldn't afford Christmas gifts, or even a tree. But your grandma always found a way to make the holiday magical—"

"Mom," I started, hoping to cut her off. My heart stuttered at the mention of Grandma, and a memory struck me. I was six and tucked snugly beside Grandma in my twin bed on Christmas Eve. She'd promised to cuddle with me until I fell asleep, but I was so excited for Santa that I couldn't get my eyes to close. So Grandma read *The Night Before Christmas* at least a dozen times, missing most of the holiday party that Mom and Dad were hosting downstairs. Finally, when my eyes drooped, she slipped from the covers, whispering, "Listen for Santa's sleigh bells tonight, my sweet girl. They'll jingle through your dreams." Later, as I glided into sleep, I was sure I heard them chiming softly through the swirling snow.

Grandma and I had shared the same pointed chin, dark hair, and sharp gray eyes, and back when I was little, the same quirky giggle that Dad called the "turkey gobble." Grandma used to say that the two of us were kindred spirits. "We go together like marshmallows and chocolate." She'd laugh and pat her soft, huggable belly, adding, "I'm the marshmallow, of course."

Remembering made an ache start in my chest. I tried not to think about her this time of year, because if I did, it usually ended in waterworks. Without Grandma, Christmas didn't feel right anymore. Now I suddenly wanted more than anything for this conversation with Mom to be over, before she brought more memories to the surface.

"I do actually have homework to do, you know." I hadn't meant it to come out sounding so obnoxious, and I cringed.

Mom opened her mouth to argue, but at that second, Dad blew in through the door, declaring he needed more extension cords, and Mom dropped the subject. As I climbed the stairs to my bedroom, there was a sinking in my stomach as I thought back to Dad's disappointed face. I didn't want to let him down, but I couldn't pretend to be someone I wasn't, either. I just wish my conscience understood that.

Chapter Three

"Well, if it isn't Anti-Claus!"

I glanced up from my camera lens to see Alejandro—Alex—Perez waving from Cocoa Cravings, a cup of hot chocolate in his hand. Mom and Dad had let me off work early from the photo booth so that I could go find a gift for Nyssa, since our first Secret Santa gifts were due tomorrow. So far, though, I'd completely avoided shopping, opting to take photos instead. I sighed, reluctantly left my camera dangling around my neck, and headed in Alex's direction. My mom may have dropped the subject of the Holly Jolly House for the time being, but there was another, much more persistent champion of Christmas pestering me now: Alex.

"Hello," I said to him, playing up the annoyance in my voice for all it was worth. It was no use. He was still smiling, completely immune.

"Can I just say, I *love* that I bring out the grouch in you." His eyes glinted teasingly. "Here." He handed me the hot chocolate. "I call this one the Cocoa of Christmas Past."

"Clever," I quipped. "But if you expect me to take a sip and start sobbing over the year I didn't get that vampire doll I wanted, you'll be disappointed."

For the last two evenings that I'd worked at the North Pole Wonderland with my parents, Alex had been dauntlessly trying to sway me with different hot cocoa flavors. Tuesday, it was Cinna-more Hot Chocolate, yesterday Pumpkin Perfection, and now this.

"Strange. I would've pegged you for a zombie type," he said, unfazed. Zombies *were* way cooler than vampires, but I wasn't about to admit he'd guessed right.

It was odd, the way we'd fallen into this easy banter, especially since we were such complete opposites. I'd amped up my snarkiness at first, thinking it would scare him off. If anything, though, it seemed to make him more persistent, which was surprising, a little annoying, but also, I had to grudgingly admit, entertaining.

I sat down at one of the café tables, took a sip of his latest concoction, and shook my head as syrupy, bittersweet chocolate coated my tongue. "Sorry." I handed the cup back to him. "Too chocolaty."

"Now I *know* there's something deeply wrong with you," Alex said. "How can *anything* be too chocolaty?"

"*Está bien*, Alejandro," a deep, rusticated voice called from behind the store counter, and I saw Alex's grandfather smiling at us. "Not everyone likes so much sweetness all at once," he said. "Maybe Emery likes more of a challenge for her taste buds."

"Thanks, Señor Perez," I said, then gave Alex a look of triumph. "See? Even your grandpa knows it's pointless."

"He didn't say 'pointless.'" Alex set my cup behind the counter, then sat down across from me. "He said 'challenge.' And I'm up for it." His eyes stayed on mine longer than I expected, and I felt a confusing flutter in my stomach and dropped my eyes.

"So," he said, motioning to my camera, "I saw you taking pictures out there on the concourse. You looked completely absorbed."

"Yeah, that happens." I blushed. I hadn't realized he'd been watching me, and suddenly, I felt inexplicably self-conscious. I tended to lose track of everything when I was taking pictures. But I didn't usually have an audience while I worked. As my mom always told me when she was photographing weddings, baby showers, and other big events, "It's a photographer's job to capture candid truths, and the best way to do it is to make sure people forget you're there."

"Will you show me what you were taking pictures of?" Alex asked. "I'd love to see."

"I don't know . . ." I hesitated. My pictures felt so personal, like a piece of myself. Aside from my parents, Jez was the only one I'd ever shown them to.

"Oh, come on. You've insulted my hot chocolate four times in a row now." He gave me a mock-wounded look. "It's the least you can do."

I laughed. He had a point. "Okay. *If* I can get my viewing function to work. It's been conking out on me lately." I turned on my camera, a worn-out digital my mom had given me when she got impatient with its unpredictable breakdowns. I tried to handle it as gently as possible, but it was a moody old thing, and I'd been trying to save up money for a new one. Tonight, though, my camera seemed to be feeling cooperative, and the photos I'd taken popped up in the viewing screen right away.

"Here you go," I said, holding out the camera to him. He studied the pictures. One was of a mom and her little girl arguing as they carried bags of Toys for Tots donations. Another was of a crying baby pulling at the collar of a too-tight holiday jumper. There were about a dozen more, all of people frowning, babies crying, people arguing and looking exhausted.

"Wow," Alex said quietly. "These are amazing photos. I mean, your perspective is great, and I love the unusual angles you used."

"Thanks." My face warmed with pleasure at the compliment.

Then he looked up from the camera, studying me. "But . . . there's not a smiling face in here."

"Exactly! And *that's* what I hate about the holidays. All the stress and disappointments. I've captured the proof of that right here." I patted my camera.

"You make it sound so depressing," he said.

"It is!" I cried. "Christmas shopping brings out the worst in everyone. Take me! I'm supposed to be getting a Secret Santa gift for Nyssa right now, but instead, I'm here, talking to you! That's how much I hate Christmas shopping!" My stomach dropped as soon as the words left my mouth. "Sorry," I added quickly. "I didn't mean that spending time with you is—"

"Awful?" he finished for me. I expected him to look hurt, but to my surprise, he laughed instead. "I know you didn't. Grumpy might be your MO, but I don't take it personally." He leaned toward me. "*And* . . . you're going to be eternally grateful to me for giving you a gift idea for Nyssa."

I sighed. "Unless you have a Prada bag you'd like to donate to the cause, I doubt it."

"A girl who has everything doesn't want *more* of everything," Alex said. "The key is to give her something she'd never expect."

I threw up my hands. "It's supposed to be some sort of food, and all I've ever seen her eat are salads and veggie wraps."

He raised an eyebrow, then motioned me toward the back of Cocoa Cravings. "Come with me."

"Why?" I asked, eyeing him suspiciously.

He smiled. "It's a stretch for you, but you're going to have to trust me on this."

"Okay," I said. "But I reserve the right to boycott anything involving frosting or sprinkles."

"Fair enough." Alex laughed and tossed me an apron, which hit me square in the face. "Now suit up. It's time to get your bake on."

"Cookies?" I asked doubtfully when Alex divulged his plan. "Nyssa probably hates cookies."

Alex laid out flour, butter, and eggs on the counter. "Nobody hates cookies. If they say they do, they're in denial. Besides," he added, setting a bag of chocolate chunks on the counter, "I was born in Oaxaca, Mexico, and my family comes from a long line of chocolate makers. I bet Nyssa's never had Oaxacan chocolate gingerbread cookies before. They're special."

I rolled my eyes. "Come on. Chocolate is chocolate."

"Shhh." He glanced over his shoulder. "If Abuelo hears you say that, he'll kick you out of his kitchen." He motioned to a sign hanging on the wall above the ovens, which read OH DIVINE CHOCOLATE, WE GRIND IT ON OUR KNEES, WE BEAT IT WITH OUR HANDS IN PRAYER, AND WE DRINK IT WITH OUR EYES LIFTED TO THE HEAVENS. "See? In Oaxaca, chocolate is almost sacred. Abuelo still makes ours by hand."

Alex pointed to a straw mat on the floor toward the back of the kitchen. On it sat a low, rectangular stone table alongside what looked like a long stone rolling pin without handles. "This is a *metate*," he explained. "Where we grind the cocoa beans by hand. Most chocolate makers use machine grinders these days, but Abuelo does things the old-fashioned way. It's been a tradition in our culture for hundreds and hundreds of years. He says it's his legacy to pass it down to me."

Alex's story was fascinating, but I felt a sudden heaviness as a memory of Grandma came rushing back to me.

"It's my legacy to you," she'd said that day so long ago in the hospital, slipping her favorite holiday necklace from over her head. It had a Christmas tree charm that opened to reveal an intricate diorama of Victorian villagers ice-skating across a tiny, quaint pond. The necklace had always intrigued me, and I loved sitting in Grandma's lap cradling the locket, imagining the tiny scene coming to life in some magical *Nutcracker*-esque way.

"My locket is yours," she'd said, "along with my Christmas spirit." Her silvery hair fanned over the pillow until it seemed to disappear into it, almost translucent. "Keep it alive for me, will you?"

She'd hugged me then and held the locket out to me. But how could I possibly take it? She'd never spent a Christmas without it, and for her to let it go would make everything too final, too permanent. Something I couldn't accept. I'd jerked away, and the necklace dropped to the bed as I left the room, crying. When Mom brought me back into the room a little while later, the locket was nowhere to be seen. I knew I'd let

Grandma down, but it was a legacy I couldn't accept. Not then. Not ever.

"Em?"

I startled at the sound of my name and blinked to see Alex watching me, concern in his eyes. "Sorry," I stammered. "I was zoning."

He nodded. "Where'd you go? It didn't look like someplace happy."

"Nowhere I feel like talking about," I said, a little too abruptly.

"Fair enough," he said quietly. "Maybe you'll tell me sometime, when you're ready."

I dropped my eyes, searching for a change of subject. "So . . . do you ever go back to visit?" I asked as he handed me a measuring cup. "To Mexico, I mean?"

"We still have a lot of family there, and my parents try to take me every few years," he said. "So many people in Mexico have so little, and that's hard to see. But still, I love going. Everything seems brighter there than here, even the flowers, the sun, and the sky. And walking down the streets, you can smell chocolate on the wind."

He grinned, then leaned forward, his arm brushing my shoulder, and I caught my breath as his face came within inches of mine. I flushed. Oh no . . . what was he doing? He couldn't possibly be trying to flirt, could he? His touch was warm and unexpected, and surprised me so much that I pulled back awkwardly, almost knocking over a bag of flour in the process.

"S-sorry," I stammered, righting the bag.

He shrugged. "I just need the ginger, that's all." He reached around me to get it from the counter, while I busied myself feeling like a complete idiot. Of course he needed the ginger. That was all. Phew.

"What?" he asked, picking up on my awkwardness.

I stared at him, then giggled more out of relief than anything else. "Nothing."

"Good," he said, setting some vanilla on the counter, too. "Now that that's settled, can we bake?"

I nodded. "I'm not great at baking, though," I admitted. "It's not my specialty."

"That's okay, because it's mine," he said. "I'll teach you."

And for the next hour, that's what he did. He helped me blend the ingredients into a big mixing bowl, all the while sprinkling in little dashes of cayenne pepper or cinnamon. I felt like I was fumbling every step of the way, but Alex was so relaxed that soon I got comfortable, too. There was simple confidence in the way he moved around the kitchen, and the affection he had for chocolate showed in the way he handled it—carefully, with an air of respect. It wasn't until after he declared the dark brown batter ready that I realized that we hadn't looked at a recipe even once.

After the cookies were out of the oven and cooled, Alex pulled out a bag of cookie-decorating supplies. "Now, I know you said no frosting or sprinkles. But they won't be finished without you adding a touch of your style." He waved. "I'll be back in a few minutes. I'm going to help Abuelo clean the tables out front."

I stared at the people-shaped gingerbread cookies in front of me, resolved to avoid any Christmassy type of cuteness. Then, inspiration struck, and I smiled in spite of myself. Reaching for a bag of colorful candy, I got to work.

Ten minutes later, Alex came back into the kitchen. I held up the baking sheets proudly, and he burst out laughing. "They've definitely got style," he said.

I nodded. "Nyssa style." I'd used gumdrops and candy beads to create gingerbread cookies that looked as un-Christmassy as possible. Each of them was dressed in a telltale glee club uniform, with treble clefs emblazoned on their shirts. I'd used black sprinkles to make little music notes popping out of their mouths. I'd even taken a chance and given one cookie Nyssa's long blond hair and blue eyes. "You said to give her something she'd never expect."

"You definitely managed that, no question about it." He glanced back as a bell jingled from the counter out front. "Abuelo ran over to the food court for a sec, so I've got to get this customer."

"I can help, too," I offered, following him through the kitchen door.

As soon as I caught sight of the customer, my heart leapt to my throat. There at the counter, wearing a crumpled olive-green safari jacket, was Sawyer.

"Hey," he said in that slightly distracted, aimless tone he had.

He gave a single nod to Alex, and then his eyes flicked to me. "Emily, right?"

My insides shrunk with disappointment. I shouldn't have expected him to know my name. Still, though, I'd hoped . . .

"Um. It's, it's . . ." *Come on,* I thought as my racing pulse left me completely tongue-twisted. *It's your name for crying out loud. Spit it out.* "It's Emery!" I smiled in relief and said a silent thank-you to the fates that I'd changed out of my elf costume before I'd gone on my Nyssa-gift mission.

"Right. Emery." His eyes shifted to my ears. An amused, slightly puzzled expression flitted across his face. "You work at the mall?" The word "mall" fell flat, like it was almost too boring to bear saying. "I thought all Undergrounds hated this place."

"I *do* hate it! I wouldn't be caught dead working here." It was an automatic response, one I would've instantly given to anyone who ever would've pegged me for a mall groupie. As soon as I said it, though, Alex shot me a questioning look, and my face blazed, because technically, what I'd said wasn't exactly true anymore. "I mean, not *here* here," I blabbered, motioning to

Cocoa Cravings. "But, you know, anywhere . . . in the mall."
Cripes, I was digging myself in deep with this one. "Alex was
just helping me with some Secret Santa stuff here tonight."

"Oh, that." Sawyer rolled his eyes. "Such a waste of energy."
He swept a lock of bangs out of his eyes, and I could practically
hear my soul sighing as he did. "I'm so much better at brainstorming songs than gift ideas. I figured out a solution to that
problem, though."

I was about to ask what he meant when Alex cleared his throat
loudly, gesturing to the menu on the blackboard behind him.
"So, what can I get for you?"

"Oh, right," Sawyer said. "I'll take two large Cinna-mores,
with extra marshmallows, chocolate shavings, and whipped
cream. And I need them in to-go cups."

"Coming right up," Alex said, and turned to the enormous
brass dispensers lined up behind him, each one keeping a different type of hot chocolate warm and ready for serving.

"So you like hot chocolate?" I asked Sawyer.

"Not so much. But my mom asked me to grab some for her
and my grandma. Gran loves this place."

"That's so nice of you." I smiled.

He leaned forward, catching his reflection in the shiny side of one of the dispensers. He adjusted the angle of his hat, then turned back to me and shrugged. "It gave me an excuse to get out of the house so I could pick up some new music for the band from High Notes." He nodded toward High Notes, the music store next door.

I was about to ask about the music when Alex set the hot chocolates beside the cash register, and Sawyer's attention turned to paying. He thanked Alex just as a buzzer went off in the kitchen.

"I'll get that. Those are probably the pastries Abuelo was working on earlier." Alex gave Sawyer a quick wave, then headed for the kitchen, adding, "See you in history tomorrow."

Sawyer nodded, and turned to me. "Catch you at school?"

"Definitely," I said, smiling. It could've been my imagination, but I thought his eyes held mine for one extra meaningful second before he turned toward the concourse. I watched him as he walked away, my heart hammering happily, then went to find

Alex. He was unloading the pastries onto a cooling rack, and he glanced up at me with curiosity.

"Are you okay?" he asked. "Your face is redder than Rudolph's nose."

"It is not." I tried to sound as nonchalant as possible while simultaneously worrying over just how ridiculous I *had* actually looked. "And could you please not compare me to reindeer . . . ever?"

Alex scoffed at that, handing me a pastry box to put Nyssa's cookies in. "Fine, if you're going to be touchy about it. You just don't seem like the blushing type."

"I'm not." My face tingled with heat as I gingerly placed the cookies in the box and reached for the red cellophane paper. "Usually. It's just that . . ." I hesitated. Was I actually considering telling Alex about my crush on Sawyer? Jez was the only person I'd ever admitted it to. Alex couldn't possibly be interested in hearing about my wannabe love life. Then again, if we were going to be hanging out at the mall most days, he'd figure it out sooner or later anyway. "It's just that . . . maybe I have a little bit of a thing for Sawyer. There. I said it. Happy now?" He shrugged, and I rolled my eyes. "Oh, right. You're *always* happy."

"Not always," he said casually. "So, do you hang out with Sawyer a lot?"

"Um, well, Jez and I hang around in his group at school. But I don't usually talk to him. Ever, actually. Tonight was sort of a first." I cringed, not believing I'd admitted that, too. Why did Alex make me spill the truth like this?

"Huh." He nodded. "Then it's more of a worship-from-afar sort of thing?"

I gritted my teeth in irritation. "*No.* It's way more than that."

"Easy there." He held up his hands with a half smile. Then he shrugged, frowning slightly. "But if he doesn't know who you are, then how can he like the real you?"

"What do you mean?"

"You lied to him about working at the mall," he said quietly.

"So? He wouldn't understand. He'd never let his parents force *him* into anything he didn't believe in. He's too original for that."

"You seem to have him pegged pretty well, considering you only talked to him for the first time ever five minutes ago."

I glared at Alex. "Ooh. Why do you have to be so . . . so aggravating?"

He laughed. "What can I say? It's a gift."

"So what if we haven't had a ton of one-on-one time together? I see him every day in homeroom and at lunch. That's plenty of time for me to get a read on him." I blew out a frustrated breath. "And I *don't* want him to see me as a total sellout."

At that moment, Alex's *abuelo* came into the kitchen. "*Ahora,* time to close up shop." He smiled at me. "*Buenas noches,* señorita."

"Good night, Señor Perez." I picked up Nyssa's pastry box, then waved to him before Alex walked me through the front of the shop. As the two of us stood under the shop's awning, Alex studied me with that half-amused, half-baffled expression on his face that I was coming to realize he reserved especially for me.

"By the way. Not everyone who works at the mall is a sellout." There was a defensiveness to his voice I'd never heard before, and I felt a stab of guilt.

"I didn't mean you," I said quietly.

"I know. But doesn't hiding a part of yourself sort of make you one?" I frowned, wanting to argue, but before I could, he nudged me. "Let's not end the night fighting, okay?" He held up a gold bow. "Here. The finishing touch." He stuck the bow on top of the package for Nyssa, then smiled. "Wrapped and ready to go."

I wanted to stay annoyed with him, in his cheery, know-it-all glory. But he sort of saved the day with Nyssa's gift idea, even if he was clueless when it came to Sawyer.

"Thanks for your help," I said, using every ounce of willpower to make my voice sound peacemaking. "I never thought I'd say this, but it was fun. Baking with you."

"Of course it was," he said. "You're an elf. Baking's in your blood."

"Argh!" I elbowed him. "Would you *quit* calling me an elf?"

"Okay," he said with a mischievous grin, "but how else do you explain the ears?"

"Wha—?" I reached up to my ears in confusion, then froze when I felt something plastic and pointy protruding from my hair. "Omigod. I forgot to take them off!" And Sawyer had seen me in them! So *that's* why he'd been staring at my ears! "Why didn't you tell me?" I cried.

"I just did." Alex laughed. "Besides, they look good on you."

I made a lunge for him, but just as I did, he pulled the gates closed over the storefront. "See you at school, Emery Elf," he called from safety on the other side.

I yanked off the ears and stormed through the concourse. But by the time I reached the North Pole Wonderland, I was giggling in spite of myself. *Boys,* I thought with a shake of my head, *when you're not crushing on them, you want to strangle them.*

Chapter Four

Friday morning when I got to Mrs. Finnegan's class, I saw a purple gift bag in the center of my desk. On nearly every desk in the room were gifts in various shapes and sizes, wrapped in bright paper or sitting in patterned gift bags.

Even though I warned it ahead of time not to do it, my heart sped up. *Traitor*, I thought. No matter how much I argued with myself that I didn't need or want a present, the second it was in front of me, all I wanted to do was rip it open. I lifted the bag. A raven-shaped tag dangled from one of its handles, and when I

55

flipped it over, I read: For a girl full of sweetness and bite. Like this candy. From, Guess who?

Intrigued, I reached through a mound of silver tissue paper into the bag. I pulled out a crinkly package and found myself smiling at the pink skull and crossbones on its front. It was a supersized pack of Venom candy—my favorite. I popped a piece into my mouth just as Nyssa walked into the class.

I held my breath as she approached her desk, where her red-and-gold present sat waiting. Before the bell rang, I'd enlisted Jez's help, having her put the present on Nyssa's desk for me so that no one would guess who it was really from.

Nyssa picked it up, weighing it in her hands. "Ooh, it's heavy."

"Watch out," Vince, sitting in the desk beside her, snorted, "it could be a nasty fruitcake."

"Shh." Nyssa stifled a giggle as she started ripping off the cellophane. "Whoever gave it to me will hear you."

I cringed as Nyssa lifted the lid of the pastry box. She pulled out the gingerbread version of herself and stared.

"Whoa. Definitely homemade." I held my breath, trying to decipher her tone. It could go either way . . . offended or impressed. She tilted her head, holding up the cookie to the light. "Hey. I think it's supposed to be . . . me!" I mentally prepared myself to hear a snarky critique. Then—shocker—she bit the gingerbread girl's head clean off. "It's delicious!" she said, cookie crumbs flying out of her mouth.

If my mouth hadn't been puckered around my candy, it would've hit the floor.

"Mmmm," Nyssa mumbled, relishing the cookie, her eyes closed in pleasure. "I haven't had homemade cookies since my nanny quit."

"You're kidding," Vince said. "Your mom never baked you cookies before?"

"Not even once," she said. "We practically live on takeout. I get so sick of it."

Wow. Two Nyssa revelations in less than two minutes. I wasn't entirely sure how to process what I'd overheard, but there was definitely a question forming in my mind. Was there more to her than the aura of privileged aloofness she gave off?

By the time Mrs. Finnegan walked in to start class, I was relieved, and secretly pleased, to see Nyssa scarfing down her third cookie. Alex had been right. Giving Nyssa something she never expected had been a clever idea, and it felt good watching her enjoy the cookies we'd worked so hard to make.

Not everyone in our class fared so well with their gifts, though. Vince was the one who ended up with a fruitcake. The gourmet cheese and sausage gift basket that Sawyer had gotten loomed at least a foot above his head. It was absurdly big, and Sawyer was inspecting it with mild curiosity. He pulled a French-labeled container from the basket.

"This could be a great place to find song titles," he said to his friend and bandmate Gabe. "Maybe 'Rancid Cheese' or 'Look What the Rat Dragged In'?"

"Brilliant," Gabe said appreciatively, scribbling the titles down in his notebook.

"They are, aren't they?" Sawyer laughed at his own joke, and I did, too.

Sawyer glanced in my direction and nodded, a smile playing at the corners of his mouth. I blushed like mad, then looked away. He was being a pretty good sport over a gift so obviously wrong for him, and I couldn't help wishing (again) that I'd pulled his name out of the Santa hat. He needed a Secret Santa who *knew* him, like mine, it seemed, knew me.

Which brought me back to the mystery surrounding *my* gift. I spent most of class wondering who my Secret Santa was. Sure, I could usually be seen unwrapping a Venom in between classes or after lunch, but somebody who noticed and remembered such a small detail must be noticing *me*.

Then lightning struck. I might not know who my Secret Santa was yet, but I had a perfectly logical explanation for how they'd found me such a perfect gift. They'd had help from someone, and I knew who.

"Me?" Jez blinked blankly. "I didn't help anyone with your gift."

I narrowed my eyes at her. "Are you sure?"

She shook her head adamantly over her samosas as the cafeteria around us buzzed with lunchtime chat. None of us Undergrounds sat at the tables. Instead, we always sprawled across the stage at the far end of the cafeteria. It was less crowded there and gave us a great view of the other tables. I could see

Nyssa chatting away with her glee club friends, and Alex munching on a sandwich and laughing with some kids I didn't recognize.

"You know I'm a terrible liar," Jez said now. "If your Secret Santa had come to me, I'd spill the beans to you in seconds."

It was true. Jez had never been good at keeping secrets from me. "Weird," I said as I munched my sandwich. "So, if you weren't involved, then who?"

Jez shrugged. "Maybe Lyra? Or Rafael? They're both in your class."

Lyra and Rafael were part of the Undergrounds, but I didn't know either of them that well. They were a couple and spent most of their time holding hands and whispering to each other in delirious adoration.

"Maybe," I said. "But they never seem to take their eyes off each other for long enough to notice much of anything, least of all what kind of candy I like."

"Well, then, what about . . . ?" Jez nodded her head in the direction of Sawyer, who was sitting off toward the edge of stage right, bending over some sheet music with Gabe.

"I wish. But as of last night, he didn't even know my name. I'm not optimistic." I sighed, looking at that intense, reflective expression on Sawyer's face. Man, if only he'd look at me like that. Suddenly, as if by magic, he did. He lifted his head, his eyes met mine in this take-my-breath-away glance, and he waved me over to him. "Omigod." I clutched Jez's hand. "He wants to talk to me."

"Then why are you still sitting here?" Jez hissed in my ear, nudging me with her shoulder. "Go! Go!"

I crossed the stage on shaky legs, hoping I wouldn't botch this the way I'd botched last night's confab.

"Um, you wanted to see me?" I stammered.

"Oh. Yeah." Sawyer's eyes drifted back to the music again. "Emery." My name rolled off his tongue like it was the start of a song. So dreamy. "I heard you're a photographer?"

Photographer. Wow. Nobody had ever made it sound so serious, so professional before.

When I found my voice, I said, "I like to take pictures. Yes."

He nodded without looking up. "Gabe and I were talking, and we need a photo for the cover of the new CD we're putting together. Something dark, wintry-looking but with a punk edge. Do you think maybe you could come up with something? We want to sell copies of the CD at our concert in a couple weeks."

"Sure," I blurted quickly, then cursed myself for sounding so eager. "I'd love to."

"Great." He smiled. "So . . . see you."

"See you," I said, backing up across the stage. I couldn't stop grinning. Sawyer had gone from not knowing my name to asking me to help with his band's CD. *That* was progress.

I spent the rest of the day brainstorming ideas for Sawyer's CD cover. It took me twice as long as usual to walk home from school, because I was snapping pictures the whole way down Main Street. My plan was to take a picture of some ordinary wintry scene, like a wreath on someone's door, or a pine tree covered in snow, and then I could play with it on the computer, darkening the exposure, creating more of a ghostly feel.

By the time I turned onto Willow Court, I'd taken a few dozen pictures, and I was anxious to upload them to see what I had to work with. But when I spotted our house, my high spirits sank with embarrassment.

The Holly Jolly House was fully operational, and already a throng of moms and their little kids were oohing and aahing at the prancing, singing animatronic animals. The thousands of lights Dad had strung didn't have much of an effect in broad daylight, but that didn't seem to dampen this group's enthusiasm.

I tried to slip into the backyard unnoticed, but suddenly one of the little girls swiveled her head toward me.

"Look!" she cried, beaming and pointing. "It's Emery Elf! I saw you at the mall!" At least five other kids turned to wave at me, but then the girl's eyes narrowed with suspicion. "Wait a second. How come you're not wearing your elf clothes? And . . ." She tilted her head. "Your ears aren't pointy anymore!"

"That's because I'm not an elf," I said distractedly. I didn't even think about what I was saying, or who I was saying it to. The only thought I had was that I wanted to get inside as quickly as possible and avoid this whole conversation. "I only pretend to be one at the mall. I'm not the real deal."

The girl's eyes widened. "But if you're not a real elf, then the Santa at the mall isn't . . ." Her voice died away as her face crumpled into tears. Her mom rushed over, giving me a mildly scolding glance.

"That's not what I said," I started to protest, but then suddenly Dad was at my side.

"Who wants a candy cane?" he said, and instantly, kids surrounded him, all smiles once again. Except for the one little girl, who was still crying.

"Sorry, Dad," I mumbled. "I didn't mean to—"

"We'll talk about it later," he said in a tired, disappointed voice. "Go on inside."

As I walked away, I could hear the mom saying, "It's all right, Sophie. Sometimes elves have secret identities when they're around humans. See, they have magical powers that make them look like humans . . ."

I shut the front door and heaved a sigh, convinced I was going to hear it from Dad as soon as he came inside. Sure enough, not ten minutes later, he tracked me down in Mom's studio, where I'd started uploading my photos.

"Emery." He shook his head, exasperation in his eyes. "How could you do that?"

"It just slipped out!" I cried. "I was thinking about something else."

He frowned. "Look, I don't know what sort of phase this is you're going through, but no matter how you feel about Christmas, it's not fair for you to ruin it for children!"

A pit formed in my stomach, and I turned back to the computer, unable to meet his eyes. "I don't think I really ruined it," I reasoned softly. "I mean, I didn't sign on to stay in elf mode all the time. Doing it at the mall is bad enough."

"Emery," Dad said quietly, "I didn't force you to help out with the Holly Jolly House. But you still have to respect what it means. I don't just decorate for us. I decorate for the families of Fairview so that everyone can enjoy some holiday spirit."

I gaped at him. "No way am I dressing up as an elf in our own house!"

"I'm not asking you to. But I am asking you to keep your

attitude in check when you're around the families who stop by to enjoy the decorations."

"Fine," I muttered, "but I don't see the point. Every kid realizes it's a sham sooner or later anyway."

Dad sucked in a breath, as if I'd physically wounded him. "I'm so sorry to hear you say something like that." He turned toward the door, then paused to add, "Believing is never a sham."

The door clicked shut, and I slumped over the keyboard. Then, even though I knew it would only seal the deal on my bad mood, I reached into my messenger bag and pulled out the picture that I'd carried with me everywhere for the last four years.

The technique in the photo wasn't great. It was slightly out of focus and off center. But there we were—Grandma and nine-year-old me in front of our ginormous three-story Christmas tree, smiling like two slap-happy buffoons. I still remembered that day like it was yesterday—the caramelly roasted nuts that stuck to my teeth like taffy, Grandma singing "Silver Bells" at the top of her lungs while I giggled, the warmth of her wispy-thin hand as it held mine.

I brushed a finger lightly over her face, recognizing a flicker of myself in her eyes and mouth. Hanging around her neck was the Christmas locket. With a flash of shame, I realized I didn't even know what had happened to it. I shook my head, getting a quivery, close-to-crying feeling. Biting my lip, I resolved not to give into it, then put the photo away.

If Grandma had been here, she probably would've given me a piece of her mind, too.

Because the truth was, if I hadn't been so caught off guard by—what was her name again?—Sophie and her questions, I probably would've told her some spur-of-the-moment story about being an "Elf Undercover." I didn't want little kids disillusioned because of me, either.

I wanted to be furious at Dad. But it was hard to stay mad at him for long. Mom teasingly called him a "boy in man's clothing," and in a lot of ways, he was. He laughed hysterically at *Looney Tunes*, and could be caught dunking Oreos in milk for breakfast. The Holly Jolly House had been his and Grandma's idea in the first place, not Mom's, and although she helped him with it as much as she could, I'm not sure she loved it the way he did.

I hated him being disappointed in me, but sooner or later, he'd have to realize how different I was from him. I was getting older, and there were some childish things I didn't need anymore. Christmas was one of them.

Chapter Five

The Secret Santa mystery deepened on Wednesday afternoon, before my least favorite class: phys ed.

Jez and I walked into the locker room to change into the horrifyingly ugly gym pants and tees we were forced to wear each week. Then we both stopped short.

On the bench in front of my locker was a small box wrapped in cute zombie paper and tied with a hot-pink ribbon. The tag had my name on it.

"I'll say this for your Secret Santa," Jez said, admiring the package. "Whoever it is has your tastes down pat."

My heart hammered as I opened the present. When I lifted the lid on the box, inside was a mug with an illustrated, sulking elf on the front. Her thick black bangs hung over one eye, and there was a broken black heart on her red turtleneck. A note taped to the mug read: *An emo elf, just for you.*

"It's perfect." I didn't even try to hide the surprise in my voice.

Jez nodded. "That mopey face is *so* you." She peered at my face, then dropped her mouth in mock shock. "Somebody call nine-one-one!" she hollered over the lockers. "Em's smiling! From a Christmas present!"

"Yes, I like the gift," I huffed, tucking the mug carefully into my messenger bag. "But it's frustrating. There's this person out there who knows so much about me, and I have no idea who she is." I paused, blushing. "Or, *he* is."

"Yeah. What will you do if it's a boy?" Jez asked, tying her running shoes. "I mean, it's like you two already have a connection. Your souls speak to each other."

I was about to roll my eyes at her when my cell phone buzzed with an incoming text message. My heart somersaulted as I read:

> Hey, Em. Got ur # from Lyra. Was late 2day so missed u in homeroom. R u around at lunch? Can we talk about pics for the CD?

"It's from Sawyer!" I said, my voice rising in a jubilant swoop.

"That sounded dangerously close to a cheerleader-ish squeal." Jez ribbed me.

I waved a dismissive hand in her face, ignoring her. "He wants to talk with me at lunch. About the CD cover."

"This could be a banner day," Jez said. "Think about it. A perfect Secret Santa gift, and Sawyer texting you . . . your relationship with him just reached a whole new level."

I scoffed. "I don't *have* a relationship with Sawyer."

"*Yet*," Jez reminded me.

The bell rang, and we headed for the door to the gym. But for the rest of class, my thoughts bounced back and forth between the cute pouty elf mug and Sawyer. Whenever I thought of either one, I smiled. I felt a heart-thrilling, toe-tingling

anticipation. It was the kind of feeling that usually meant something wonderful was about to happen.

Sitting side by side with Sawyer in the cafeteria was so perfect I
could barely breathe with the electrifying shivers shooting up
and down my spine. Our shoulders were almost brushing, and I
could smell the spiciness of his hair gel.

"This should only take a sec," I said as we waited for my tablet to pull up all the photo files.

"It's all good," Sawyer said, tucking a beautiful purpled strand
of hair behind his ear. Forget the camera. That was a view I
could stare at all day long.

"Okay," I said as the pictures popped up in a grid on the
screen. "I wasn't sure exactly what you were looking for, but you
mentioned dark, punk. So I tried a couple different things."

Sawyer swiped his finger across the screen, studying
each craggy, ice-coated tree, each windblown wreath. I'd
manipulated the exposures in most of the pictures to create a
haunted feel.

"Whoa. This one's twisted." He nodded in appreciation at a plastic Rudolph yard ornament that I'd made look skeletonized. "I didn't know you had such a dark side."

"You have no idea," I joked, trying to play the compliment off coolly while my cheeks flushed. "Most of the time I use Photoshop. But with this one, I manipulated the negative by hand, just for fun. My mom has this vintage camera that still uses thirty-five-millimeter film rolls. She taught me how to use it and develop pictures in an actual dark room."

"Huh." He nodded, but had a slightly glazed look in his eyes that made it seem like he was losing interest. "I never take pictures. I've never seen the point of reliving the past. Life's all about the present, you know?"

"Oh. Sure." I acted like I got that, even though the idea of not having pictures of friends and family from the past seemed like such a sad loss. "There's so much more you can do with pictures, though, don't you think? Create a story within a picture, add something that wasn't there before, change the feeling—"

I stopped talking when I saw his eyes suddenly freeze on the screen. He burst out laughing.

"This one." He pointed. It was a photo of a tantruming tod-dler in a Santa's hat, stomping on a present. It was one of the photos I'd taken at the mall last week. "This one's perfect. It captures everything we want to say in this album."

"Really?" My spirits lifted. So what if the photo he'd picked wasn't one of the ones I'd taken specifically *for* him? Mom was always telling me that was what happened with her customers, too. She said they always bought prints of her least favorite pho-tos. "So what is it you're trying to say?" I asked Sawyer. "In the album, I mean?"

"Didn't I tell you already?" His amber eyes settled on mine, and the air rushed out of my lungs. "We've titled it *Bah Humbug*. It's an anti-Christmas album." He motioned to Gabe and the other band members, who were sitting a few feet away, eating. "We want to speak out against the deception of the holiday. You know, the hoax of it all."

"That's unbelievable." I stared at him. "I feel the same way. That's why I took that picture! Because I get so tired of people pretending it's a season of joy when really it's a bunch of misery."

"I hear that," he said empathetically, and there was a spark of enthusiasm in his eyes that hadn't been there up until now. "And the mall is the worst. That jingly music is torture. And the people! All wearing tight smiles while underneath they're wishing they could just get the holiday season over with. The people who work there must be crazy. Or desperate. How else could they put up with the charade?"

"Yeah," I managed weakly, my stomach twisting uneasily. "I know what you mean. Of course, some of them might not have a choice."

He stared at me like I'd said the world was flat. "Everyone has a choice. Nobody just forces somebody into doing something he doesn't believe in."

"Wanna bet?" I quipped. "My parents can."

"It's obvious why," he said. "They're probably complete conformists." He glanced at me, seemingly waiting for agreement, so I quickly nodded. Of course he was right to think that. After all, he'd probably seen the Holly Jolly House. "My parents are free-bird types. They're not much into rules."

"I don't suppose they'd consider adopting?"

He smiled. "That bad, huh?"

"Not all the time. But this time of year especially."

"How come?" For the first time since we'd started talking, he looked so sincerely interested that my heart tripped with hope. Sawyer Kade wanted to know about *me*. It was enough to make me dizzy with happiness. But I had to be careful. My eyes flicked over to where Alex was sitting with his friends. I'd managed to avoid telling Sawyer about working at the mall so far, and I wanted to keep it that way. If he knew the truth, he'd think I wasn't strong enough to stand up for my beliefs. Or that I was a hypocrite. Now that we were finally talking after all the time I'd spent crushing on him from a distance, I didn't want to mess it up.

I hesitated, debating how much, if anything, I wanted to share, when suddenly, from across the cafeteria, I heard music. The lunchtime chatter trickled to whispers as four kids I recognized from the glee club danced across the room dressed as candy canes and singing "Jingle Bells" in perfect harmony. When I realized they were headed straight for us, my first instinct was to run. My second was to sink into the floor and die. Neither was possible.

When the quartet was a few feet from where Sawyer and I were sitting, they changed their tune to "We Wish You a Merry Christmas," turning all their smiling faces in Sawyer's direction. I glanced at Sawyer, who was watching the escapade with a mixture of bemusement and nonchalance. As soon as the quartet finished singing, they presented him with a bouquet of red and green balloons and candy canes.

"Let me guess," Gabe said as he walked over to inspect Sawyer's balloons. "Secret Santa strikes again?"

Sawyer glanced at the note attached to his bouquet and nodded, then shrugged. "It could've been worse. And in defense of my Secret Santa, I'm not that easy to buy for," he said good-naturedly. He turned to me. "Are you having better luck with yours?"

I nodded. "My gifts have been great so far. Although I really wasn't into the whole thing in the first place."

"Me neither," he said. "Still, though, I guess it's a good way to get to know people better." He gave his balloons a shake. "Or . . . *not.*"

The bell rang, and I felt a twinge of disappointment that our time was over so soon. We stood to throw our trash away, and then he turned back, those soulful eyes peering out at me from under his dark, jagged bangs. "That picture will be perfect for the CD cover. You totally got what I needed."

"Thanks." My blush deepened. "I'll email you the picture right now."

"Perfect. The CDs should be ready sometime next week."

"I'd love a copy," I blurted.

He smiled. "You'll be the first person I give one to."

Then he was gone in the crowd of kids shuffling out of the cafeteria, taking my heart with him.

"I can't believe it," Jez said within seconds of Sawyer being safely out of earshot. "I've never seen him look at a girl that way before. Plenty of girls look at *him* that way, but never the other way around."

Even though I wanted to be rational about this, my smile kept spreading. "I just wish I knew for sure how he felt. You know, something concrete—" I stopped midsentence and grabbed Jez's arm. "I can't believe it. She's actually wearing it!"

I motioned to Nyssa, who was a few feet ahead of us in the crowd of kids, showing off the fitted pink tee I'd slipped into her schoolbag on the way out of homeroom this morning. It was my second Secret Santa gift to her. On the front of the shirt was a quote from *Glee*'s Rachel that read: *I look forward to the day the paparazzi provokes me and I attack them.* I'd taken a risk with it, not knowing how much of a sense of humor Nyssa really had.

But as I watched, I heard her saying to Dana, one of her glee friends, "I love it! It's *so* me, don't you think?"

"I guess," Dana said lackadaisically as she fiddled with her lip gloss. "I never pictured you wearing campy TV slogans before."

"Me neither," Nyssa said with her tinkly laugh. "But it's fun. It does make me feel guilty about the Secret Santa gifts I've been giving, though. I can't get any of them right." She sighed, tucking a strand of her glossy blond hair behind her ear. "Did you see Sawyer's face in the cafeteria? He hated the singing holiday gram. I want to give him something he likes, but the problem is, I don't get Sawyer at all!"

"I do!" I blurted, and three pairs of shocked eyes turned my direction. Jez gave me a "what are you doing?" glance, and Dana's brow knitted in confusion. Nyssa gave me a slightly mystified but not unwelcoming smile. "Get Sawyer, I mean." I swallowed, pressing onward. "Look, I heard you talking about the Secret Santa thing. And . . . I know Sawyer. I could help with ideas if you want."

Nyssa breathed out a sigh of relief. "Really? That would be awesome, because I'm getting desperate."

"Yeah, the holiday gram made that loud and clear." I realized as soon as I said it that it might have been wiser to tone down my usual sarcasm.

But Nyssa's eyes widened in astonishment, and then she burst into giggles, shaking her head. "You and Sawyer must really be soul mates."

My adrenaline surged. "Wait. What do you mean?"

"Oops." She slapped her hand to her mouth in a dramatic gesture perfectly suited to stage performances. Then she leaned toward me conspiratorially. "I probably shouldn't tell you this, but it's just too perfect." She grinned gleefully and whispered, "Sawyer's *your* Secret Santa."

My breath caught. "What?" I gasped when I was finally able to talk.

Nyssa nodded. "It's true! I heard him talking about it outside Mr. Gunther's history class the other day."

My mind reeled giddily, trying to process what I'd heard. Sawyer . . . It was like a dream come true. I wanted to laugh, or dance, or shriek with joy, but then the late bell buzzed and we all jumped.

Nyssa gave a childish pout, clearly sad to be missing out on the chance to gossip more. "I have to go or Mrs. Jenkins will give me a tardy again." She waved to me and Jez as she and Dana walked away. "I'm going to pick your brain about you-know-who later!" she called over her shoulder.

I nodded, then turned to Jez, smiling dazedly.

"Sawyer's my Secret Santa." I shook my head. "That's, that's—"

"Fate," Jez finished for me.

Three hours later, I set my brand-new mug down on the counter at Cocoa Cravings and said, "Fill 'er up."

"I don't even get a 'hello'?" Alex said teasingly.

"Eh," I said in my best blasé tone. "We're past that. You don't want my 'hello' as much as you want my hot chocolate conversion, so I figured I'd cut to the chase."

"You got me there." He laughed and poured me some hot chocolate. "I call this one Caramel Crush."

I took a sip and salt crystals and caramel zinged pleasantly over my tongue. But it left a sticky, sugary coating in my mouth. "It was off to a promising start," I said. "Then it turned syrupy."

Alex sighed. "You're one tough critic."

"Sorry." I shrugged.

He grinned, then examined my mug and whistled. "That's one tough-looking elf."

A blush rose to my cheeks. "It was my second Secret Santa

gift. I got it today." I waited a beat for dramatic effect before adding, "From Sawyer."

Alex's eyes widened momentarily. "So *that's* what's behind your good mood. I thought maybe you stole all the toys from the Whos down in Who-ville on your way here or something."

I shook my head. "I'll get my Grinch on another day."

His laugh was delayed in coming, and it sounded forced. He turned to rinse out my mug at the sink behind the counter. "That's big news. How'd you find out Sawyer was your Secret Santa?"

"Nyssa's *his* Secret Santa. While I was offering to help her pick out some gifts for him, she accidentally on purpose spilled the beans," I explained. "She's stuck on the idea of the two of us being meant for each other. So is Jez."

"And you believe it, too," he said matter-of-factly as he set the clean mug in my hands.

"I—I do." My heart hammered wildly as he looked at me. "Before I knew he was my Secret Santa, it was tough to tell if I'd ever have a shot with him. I mean, I thought we'd have a connection if he ever noticed me. But now I know he's been noticing me all along." I smiled. "This changes everything."

Alex regarded the mug thoughtfully. "Look," he said finally, "I don't want to burst your bubble or anything, but what if he doesn't know you the way you think he does?"

I stared at him, feeling an itch of irritation. What did Alex know? "We both love the same music, we both hate Christmas. Plus, he knows I love Venom candy, and the mug is basically made for me."

"What if someone else is helping him pick out the gifts he's giving you? The way you're going to be helping Nyssa." His shoulders tensed, like this whole conversation was making him uncomfortable. "I'm just saying that maybe you shouldn't read too much into it."

"And maybe *you* shouldn't be so negative," I snapped, frowning. Why was he acting so weird about this? And why should his opinion matter to me, anyway? I sighed, crossing my arms. "I shouldn't have told you. I had a feeling you didn't like Sawyer."

"I like Sawyer just fine. That's not the problem."

"Then, what is?" I glared at him, waiting.

Alex blew out a breath. "Nothing. Forget it." He shrugged. "You're right. It's not any of my business." He gave me a smile. It wasn't his usual wide, easy smile, but smaller, more polite, and somehow less real. "Anyway, it's nice to see you enjoying *something* about Christmas. Finally!"

"Nuh-uh." I wagged a finger at him. "Don't even think about giving Christmas the credit for this. This is Sawyer's doing."

"Okay," he said. "I just thought if you were coming around to the idea of Christmas, it might make what I'm about to tell you easier to take."

I narrowed my eyes at him. I did *not* like the sound of this. "What are you up to? Spill it."

He held up his hands innocently. "It wasn't me, I swear. Abuelo and your dad were talking. They had it all planned out before I even got here from school."

"Had what planned?" I asked.

"Our trip into Manhattan this Saturday. Abuelo has to go to this store called Kalustyan's. That's where he does his spice shopping for the hot chocolate. It's the best place to get Pasilla de

Oaxaca chilies. Your dad thought it'd be fun for you to tag along to see the city decked out for the holidays. He said you used to go in with your grandma, but you haven't been since—"

"I can't believe this!" I interrupted, wincing at the mention of Grandma. "What, are you all conspiring against me now?"

Alex laughed. "Not conspiring. More like gently coaxing . . ."

"Ha." I rolled my eyes and glanced toward the North Pole Wonderland, where I could see my dad looking in our direction and smiling. "What happens if I refuse to go?"

"Your dad said that might happen. In which case, you'd have to work a double shift at North Pole Wonderland." Alex's eyes twinkled, and I sighed in annoyance. He was enjoying this *way* too much. "Oh, and there'd be a bonus, free photo for every customer posing with Emery the Elf."

My head dropped to the countertop as I groaned. "Fine," I muttered into the granite. "I'll go. But I still don't see what you all are hoping to prove."

Alex grinned. "That you're not as much of a scrooge as you think you are."

Chapter Six

"Okay, you did *not* tell me this trip involved delivering toys," I said as Alex and I hefted an enormous red bag out of his *abuelo*'s trunk.

"Don't worry," Alex said over the din of the traffic streaming up Third Avenue. "There aren't any chimneys involved."

"Somehow, that doesn't make me feel much better." I stepped up on the curb, almost bumping into a passerby. I wasn't used to the crowds and bustle of Manhattan.

Alex smiled, closing the trunk and joining me on the

sidewalk. "Look on the bright side. At least you don't have to wear your elf costume."

Señor Perez rolled down the passenger-side window to say good-bye. "Have fun!" he called. "I'll pick you up at Rockefeller Center at seven. Call my cell phone if you need me."

"*Sí, sí,* Abuelo." Alex waved. "*Hasta luego.*"

"Thank you!" I called into the car.

As Señor Perez pulled away from the curb, I turned toward Alex. "Seven?" I repeated skeptically. "It's going to take us four hours to deliver these presents?"

"Oh no. There's lots more torture, I mean fun, in store for you after this. Wait and see." He laughed. But when my frown didn't lessen, he gave me a nudge. "Come on, Em. You've had fun so far, haven't you?"

"Yes," I said grudgingly. I'd actually had a lot of fun. On the drive into Manhattan, Alex and I had talked nonstop, debating our different tastes in music, movies, and books. As we teased each other and argued, we kept laughing, and the hour-long car ride had flown by. There were moments, too, when Alex would catch my eye in the middle of my talking, and a sudden, inexplicable shyness came over me. It was the way he looked at me. Like he wasn't listening out of politeness but because he really wanted to hear what I had to say.

Our stop at Kalustyan's had been fascinating. We'd spent a good hour exploring the three stories of spices, dried chilies, nuts, and herbs. I'd bought a packet of loose herbs so that I could make Nyssa homemade tea sachets as my next Secret Santa gift to her. I'd heard her saying to one of her friends that she needed to stock up on tea before the glee holiday concert. Apparently, she drank it before each show to soothe her voice. And Alex assured me that Kalustyan's herbs were one of a kind.

The store was so cool. Its wonderful fusion of zesty scents had left behind traces that I still imagined smelling on the brisk winter wind. The shop's dark wooden shelves and endless aisles were full of every cooking ingredient imaginable, and it was amazing to watch Señor Perez and Alex deftly navigate the maze to find exactly what they needed. I was surprised to see Alex as confident as his grandpa in selecting perfect peppers, and I could tell he enjoyed the process just as much. He was as knowledgeable about the store as any tour guide, explaining the different uses for the spices in hot chocolate and how they altered the taste in subtle ways.

It was while in the store that something strange had happened. We were whispering as we smelled a jar of vanilla beans. But all the spices must have muddled my senses, because suddenly, I wasn't focused on the beans. I was looking at Alex's mouth, at how soft and full his lips looked. And then a thought flashed through my head. What might it be like to kiss Alex? It freaked me out enough to jerk back, knocking my head against the shelves behind me.

"Whoa," he said, laughing. "It's vanilla. It won't bite."

"I—I know," I stammered, trying to recover from what was obviously some bizarre hallucination. Of course I'd never kiss Alex. The only boy I'd ever wanted to kiss was Sawyer. I didn't even understand where that thought had come from, but I was going to forget it.

But now as Alex heaved the bag of gifts onto his shoulder and started down the sidewalk, motioning me to follow, I felt stirrings of unease again.

We turned right onto Fifty-Ninth Street, then stopped half a block down in front of the Families Together Shelter. I followed Alex up a short set of stairs and into the brick building, where a woman behind the check-in counter greeted him by name.

"You've been here before?" I whispered.

Alex nodded. "Abuelo and I stop here every time we're in the city. We always try to bring something, even if it's small." He handed me my visitor pass, and then I followed him down the hallway and into a large rec room where dozens of children were busy eating and playing.

"Look," one little boy of four or five cried happily. "It's Alex!" He slammed his little body into Alex's in a fierce hug.

"Hey, Ty!" Alex kneeled down and opened the bag, digging through it until he pulled out a present with Ty's name on it. "I brought something special for you today, bud. Merry Christmas!"

Ty's eyes lit up as he ripped off the paper to reveal a toy bulldozer. That was all it took. Within seconds, the rest of the children swarmed around us, jumping up and down for their presents, too.

Alex turned to me and, before I could protest, settled a load of presents into my arms.

"Better get started," he said. "Or they might mob you."

I glanced at the presents, hesitating. "I'm not great at this kind of thing," I started, remembering my unfortunate interactions with the kids at the mall, and the little girl, Sophie, at the Holly Jolly House. "Besides, wouldn't it be better to donate food or clothing? That's what these kids need more than anything."

Alex looked out at the expectant faces peering up at us, then at me. "Sometimes it's not about need. It's about being a kid. Just playing . . . not worrying about adult problems." He gave me an encouraging smile. "You can do this. Give it a try."

"Okay," I said warily. "But if there are tears, don't tell me I didn't warn you."

Alex shook his head, smiling and handing out gifts. "Sounds good."

I took a present from the top of my pile and read the name out loud. "Anna."

Within seconds, a knee-high girl with springy black curls was tugging at my shirt for her gift. She opened it and gave a gleeful shriek. "A Chatty Sally doll! She moves her arms and legs and"—she giggled, her eyes glowing with happiness—"even wets her diapers for real."

I laughed. The girl was so cute, and her enthusiasm contagious. "That's great." Who knew a bed-wetting doll was some girls' dream come true?

"Me next!" a boy called out, clapping his hands. "I'm Gerry."

"Gerry, okay . . ." I rummaged through the presents, looking for his, and soon I was busy handing out gift after gift, watching, fascinated, as the kids ripped open their packages and wrapping paper flew helter-skelter around the room. It was joy-infused chaos, and the expressions on the kids' faces were priceless—pure and candid.

Once my presents were all passed out, I grabbed my camera and, before I really understood what I was doing, started snapping photos. They weren't anything like the pictures I usually took. But it didn't matter. The smiles I caught on camera were just as genuine as any frowns or tears I'd ever captured on film. I swung my lens around the room, snapping away, then suddenly froze on one face.

Alex's. Wintry sunlight poured in from one of the windows, giving his espresso eyes a golden glow. His smile was bright, his tan face full of warmth. In an instant, looking through the lens, I saw him the way a stranger might've. I always thought of him as boyish, but in this light, as he interacted with the kids around him, he looked older and—shocker—kind of handsome. My heart sped up confusedly. What was going on with me today? I lowered the lens and glanced at him again, then saw to my relief that the old Alex was back.

But my cheeks were still heated when he caught my eye and walked over.

"That smile looks great on you," he said. "You should wear it more often."

"I wasn't smiling," I protested.

"Oh no?" Alex raised an eyebrow. "Well, in that case, that freaky thing you've been doing with your lips has been going on for a solid hour. You should really have it checked out by a doctor. Could be serious."

"Shut up." I tried to give him the evil eye, but ended up laughing instead.

"Time to go," he said, stuffing the empty red bag into his backpack. "I have some very important research to do on Sixtieth Street."

"*This* is your important research?" I asked. I sat at the small table with Alex, staring in awe at the enormous cup of frozen hot chocolate and the sundae the waitress had set down in front of us.

In the rainbow light cast by the dozen or so Tiffany lamps hanging randomly about the cheery café, I could see that every table at Serendipity 3 was packed with customers. Most of them were enjoying shakes, hot chocolates, or desserts that matched or even exceeded ours in size.

"Absolutely," Alex said, sticking two straws into the whipped cream peaks of our drink. "Abuelo likes to keep an eye on our competitors, and Serendipity 3 is famous for its frozen hot chocolate. We haven't tried anything like it at Cocoa Cravings yet." He leaned forward to whisper, "I wanted to do some reconnaissance first."

"There's no way you can drink all that," I challenged.

"You're right." He smiled. "You're going to help. Go ahead. Take a swig. If you like it, I won't take it personally. I promise."

"Okay, but then you let me off the hook to enjoy my sundae. Right?" He nodded, and I reached for the cup. As I did, my hand brushed against his, and a sudden bolt of electricity shot through me. Our eyes locked for a split second, and a strange expression flitted over Alex's face, like he'd felt the zing, too.

"Sorry," I blustered, dropping my eyes even as I felt him studying my face for another awkward few seconds.

Moments like this had been happening all day, but they were all wrong. If Sawyer was right for me, and he *was*, then whatever this was with Alex *had* to be wrong. So I was going to stop letting it affect me, no matter what. I shook my head to clear it, and focused on the frozen hot chocolate in front of me.

I took a sip and immediately shook my head. The drink was sweet but—"It goes against nature, drinking something that cold in the dead of winter."

"Clearly the finer points of great hot chocolate are lost on you. Hands off!" He playfully slapped my hands away and took possession of the hot chocolate again, taking a long, satisfying swig. "Ah. I have to say I'm glad Serendipity 3 is a whole state away from Cocoa Cravings. Otherwise, we might be in some serious trouble." He nodded toward my sundae. "What do you think?"

I cast a doubtful glance at my Strawberry Fields Sundae, which sat before me in pink-and-white glory. "Normally I'd never go for anything so sweet, but in honor of my favorite Beatles song and the great John Lennon, I'm going to give it a shot." I dug into the sundae and pulled out a towering spoonful of cheesecake and strawberry ice cream, then took a big bite. The lemony tartness of the cheesecake tempered the sugary sweetness of the ice cream just enough to make my mouth pucker. "Not too shabby."

"So 'Strawberry Fields Forever' is your favorite song," Alex said as I offered him a bite of the sundae. "I could see that, with all the nonconformist lyrics. 'Living is easy with eyes closed. Misunderstanding all you see.'"

The surprise on my face must have shown, because he laughed, shrugging. "What? I'm a Beatles fan, too."

"I love those lines," I said. "People going through the motions every day, not thinking about why they're doing what they're doing. If it means anything to them."

"Like what people do during the holidays?" he suggested.

"Exactly!" I cried. "Buying presents, singing the carols, blah blah blah. Maybe they're only doing it because it's what they've always done. They're used to it, and they're afraid to change."

"Or maybe because they truly do love what it means," he said. "Maybe it's not them misunderstanding. Maybe it's—"

"Me?" I finished for him. "I'm the one who's misunderstanding other people?"

Alex stared into his drink, seeming to have an internal debate about whether or not to keep going. "All I'm saying is that you're so stuck on proving how insincere people are. Maybe you're missing out on moments that *are* real." His eyes settled on my face, without a trace of their usual lightness, and I squirmed uncomfortably in my seat. "I saw you with those kids at the shelter," he said quietly. "When you let your guard down, you were different."

"You're reading into it," I said defensively, even though I had

had a great time with the kids. "I'm no ice queen whose heart is going to suddenly melt after handing out a few presents." I blew out a frustrated breath and put down my spoon, losing my appetite. "Can we drop it? Please?" I said. "I don't want to argue."

He hesitated, then looked up at me with a small, measured smile. "You're right. We have the rest of the afternoon to have fun in the city, and *you* have to make some serious headway on your sundae. Let's forget about it. Okay?"

I nodded in relief. "Okay."

We finished our treats and started the walk downtown toward Rockefeller Center. Even though it was only late afternoon, heavy snow clouds loomed over the skyscrapers, casting the sidewalks in shadowy twilight. Within a few minutes, flurries were spiraling down, coating the tips of my eyelashes. We walked west to Fifth Avenue. Sleigh bells were jingling from the horse-drawn carriages plodding around the outskirts of Central Park, and the smell of roasted nuts drifted in smoky, toffee-scented wisps on the wind. We passed FAO Schwarz, where the windows overflowed with giant wooden soldiers, nutcrackers, dolls, and every toy a child could want. The whole avenue was jam-packed with people admiring the elaborate holiday window displays in the fancy department stores.

When we reached Fifty-First Street, and Alex started to round the corner toward Rockefeller Center, I stopped in the middle of the sidewalk.

"Look," I started, my heart skittering. "I'm tinseled out. Maybe we could skip the Rockefeller Center tree?"

Alex's brow furrowed in confusion. "But that's where we're supposed to meet Abuelo. Come on. You've survived the last nine blocks, you can survive one more."

"Alex, wait—" It was on the tip of my tongue to tell him why I felt dread creeping up my spine, why the idea of seeing that enormous tree standing proud and tall above the ice skating rink made a knot tighten around my stomach. But he was already walking ahead, assuming I was behind him.

I sighed and burrowed my chin farther down into the collar of my coat, focusing on the sidewalk in front of me, thinking maybe if I kept my head down, I could avoid seeing the tree. As the skyscrapers opened onto the large square, with its flags rippling in the wind and the ice rink packed with happy skaters, the thousands of sparkling lights from the tree glimmered in the corner of my vision. Even though I didn't want to look, I knew I had to, so I slowly raised my eyes.

There was the tree, as glorious as I remembered it being when I was little, reaching toward the sky, its limbs aglow with rainbows of dazzling colors. Memories washed over me as I stretched my neck upward, feeling just as small and awestruck as I had so many years before, and before I could stop it, my eyes filled with tears.

"Em?" Alex said softly, glancing at my face in surprise and confusion. "What's wrong?"

"Forget it," I snapped, sniffing angrily and swiping at my eyes. "I told you I didn't want to come here!"

Alex frowned. "I thought you'd like to see the tree. I guess I pushed too hard . . ." His face, which had been so enthusiastic only a minute before, deflated into disappointment, and suddenly, I knew I couldn't stay angry at him.

"It's not your fault." I sighed, plunking down on one of the benches on the observation deck. "It's mine. I should have told you before, only . . . I don't like to talk about it." I reached into my bag and pulled out the photo and handed it to Alex as he sat down beside me.

"That's me and my grandma," I said quietly. "In front of the Rockefeller Christmas Tree. Four years ago."

Alex looked at the photo for a long minute. "You look so happy."

"I was. She used to bring me into the city every year to see the tree. It was our special day. We'd go see the *Radio City Christmas Spectacular* first, and then afterward, we'd eat roasted peanuts sitting right here, under the lights of the tree." I smiled, despite my trembling lips. "Christmas was her favorite time of year. She loved it more than anyone I've ever known, besides my dad. That's one of the reasons he puts up the Holly Jolly House each year. In honor of her memory."

Alex handed the photo back to me, and I stared at it, the sharpness of missing Grandma needling my heart. "So . . . what happened?"

"She got sick. Around Thanksgiving, when I was nine." I shook my head, tucking the photo back into my bag. "That was the year I wrote the shortest letter to Santa ever. I only asked for one thing. For him to make her better for Christmas." A hard laugh popped out of me. "Well, you can guess what happened. Or *didn't* happen."

"She never got better." His voice was barely a whisper.

I nodded. "That was the year I stopped believing in Santa. Or caring about Christmas." I sighed. "It's kind of funny. I've never admitted that out loud before. Not to anyone." I shrugged awkwardly, hoping to downplay the whole thing. Alex didn't buy the act, though.

His eyes were soft with sympathy. "I'm so sorry, Em." He ran his fingers through his dark hair, pausing over his next words. "But you have to know there probably wasn't anything anyone could do—"

"Sure. I know that *now*. But back then, no one could convince me of that. And afterward, it seemed like pretending to keep on believing was, well, a waste of time."

He shook his head. "There are other things to believe in this time of year. Family, kindness, love—"

"Don't you see? Those are things people should remember all year, not just when the commercials and holiday cards tell them to." I sighed. "If it only happens when it's forced, how genuine can it possibly be?"

"I don't think it's forced," Alex said. "I think it's more like a reminder, of all that's good that we forget about in the craziness of everyday life." His cell phone dinged then, and he checked it, then stood up. "That's Abuelo. He's waiting with the car on Forty-Eighth Street."

I nodded and stood up with a sigh.

"I'm sorry," Alex said as we walked to the car, giving me a concerned glance. "I should've listened when you tried to tell me you didn't want to come here—"

"No, it's fine," I said honestly. "It doesn't change anything, but"—I cast one last look back at the tree, elegant in its shimmering gown of lights—"I'm glad I saw it. It was nice to talk about my grandma again. Thank you."

He smiled as he opened the car door for me. "Anytime."

Chapter Seven

My trip into the city shadowed me for the rest of the weekend. I'd been thinking a lot more about Grandma since I'd talked about her to Alex, and the memories left me feeling vulnerable and touchier than usual.

On Sunday while working at the North Pole Wonderland, I noticed Alex looking worriedly my way across the concourse. I'd given him my usual roll of the eyes as I nodded toward the line of whining kids, trying to send him a silent message that I was fine. But we were both so busy with nonstop customers that we didn't get a chance to talk all day.

I was in such a funk that I even turned Jez down when she called to see if I wanted to watch a movie at her house Sunday night. When she asked what was wrong, I told her I didn't want to talk about it. But I knew Jez wouldn't give up so easily, so it was no surprise when I saw her standing sentinel at my locker first thing Monday morning, with a mischievous grin on her face.

"You're about to be de-funkified," she said. "Open your locker."

I gave her a questioning look but went ahead and opened it, and my heart surged with happiness. Inside was the new Sweet Garbage CD, with the photo I'd taken of the crying baby on the cover. On the back of the CD was a photo credit with my name on it! A Post-it attached to the CD read: Sorry I missed you this morning. Talk later? Sawyer.

"It looks amazing!" Jez said, peering over my shoulder as I smiled.

I nodded. "But how did he get it into my locker?"

Jez snorted. "Hello? I used your combination to open it for him? I was staked out here prepared to torture you with my poetry until you either laughed or spilled the beans." She shrugged. "You're lucky I didn't have to."

The bell rang, and as we made our way down the hallway, a couple of kids who passed us held up their copies of the CD, saying, "Cool cover, Emery. Nice pic!"

By the time I got to homeroom, I was starting to feel more like myself. I sat down, hoping that I might be able to talk to Sawyer before Mrs. Finnegan came in. He caught my eye as he walked in, giving me a heart-melting smile, but we didn't have the chance to say anything to each other.

Nyssa had texted me over the weekend asking if I could help her brainstorm Secret Santa gifts, and I'd suggested the two of us get a pass for the library to work on it. So, right after Mrs. Finnegan took attendance, Nyssa and I left for the library.

The second we walked out of the classroom, Nyssa giggled. "Did you see Mrs. Finnegan's smile when she wrote out our pass?"

I snorted. "Yeah. I could practically hear her warm, fuzzy thoughts about breaking down social barriers with her Secret Santa idea. Teachers eat up that sort of thing." I did my best impression of Mrs. Finnegan's high-pitched voice. "Oh, how sweet! The Underground and the—" I hesitated, not sure I should push my luck.

But Nyssa surprised me by finishing it for me. "Glee Princess." She flipped her hair over her shoulder and shrugged as we walked into the library. "It's okay. I've heard the nickname in the hallways." She leaned toward me. "I'm proud of it. I mean, I have a reputation to uphold, you know?"

I laughed. "Well, you pull it off well when you want to."

"Thanks," Nyssa said, smiling, as we sat down at a table. "You told me you had an idea for Sawyer's present?"

I nodded, my heart fluttering at hearing his name. "Well, you know he and Gabe are always working on lyrics for their songs? So what about giving him some composition sheets?"

Nyssa's eyes lit up. "That's perfect! I can have my mom take me to High Notes after school today."

"Wait a sec," I said. "This one's supposed to be a homemade gift, remember?"

Nyssa shrugged, giving me the smile I'd seen her use with teachers to butter them up when she wanted an extension on an overdue project. "Yeah, but the thing is, I don't really do homemade . . ."

I slapped some blank sheets of paper down on the table. "You do today."

She raised one slender eyebrow. "Whoa. I don't remember ordering any blunt with a side of bossy." She looked at me for one long minute, as if she expected her comment to scare me off. For most of the student body at Fairview, it probably would've worked.

But I looked at her, undaunted, and shrugged. "Subtle's not part of my vocabulary." Her eyes widened, and then, as much to my surprise as hers, we broke into laughter.

"Okay, so maybe I can tone down the bossiness a bit," I said when I'd caught my breath. "But *you* need to get in touch with your DIY side."

She blew out a breath. "I wish I had one. My mom loves to say, 'Why DIY when you can buy?'" She blushed. "I know how that sounds, believe me. But the gifts I've been getting from my Secret Santa are so unique. This morning I found a bag of home-made herbal teas in my cubby in the glee practice room." She smiled, reaching into her bag to show me one of the sachets, and I pretended like I'd never seen them before in my life. "It was such a thoughtful gift. I hoped I could do something cool like that for Sawyer, too."

My face warmed at the compliment, but I tried to keep my expression unmoving so I wouldn't give anything away.

"The thing is," Nyssa continued, "I'm not much good at arts and crafts stuff. My mom never even let me have markers when I was little. She was too scared I'd draw on the Bugatti sofa." She giggled, then whispered, "It would have felt fantastic to draw on it."

I laughed. Who knew the Glee Princess was a closet rebel? "Before you go Picasso on your mom's furniture, maybe give the composition sheets a try? With all the singing you do, I'm sure you can figure out how to draw some music staffs, right?"

She stared at the paper, then bit her lip. "It could look completely dumb when I'm finished."

"Or it could look amazing," I said, checking my watch. "We still have a while before we have to get back to class. I can help. I mean, he *is* my Secret Santa, so it's the least I can do."

She smiled in relief. "Thanks. That would be great."

"Now that we've got that settled..." I pulled some thin-tipped markers out of my bag. "Markers, meet Nyssa. Nyssa, meet markers."

Nyssa rolled her eyes but took the markers, and we bent our heads over the paper together.

By the time the bell rang for lunch, the gloom I'd felt earlier had lifted completely. I'd had fun working with Nyssa on Sawyer's gift, and now she had a dozen composition sheets finished and tied with a red Christmas ribbon.

As I walked down the hall to get my lunch bag, I was so absorbed in imagining the smile Sawyer would have on his face when he unrolled the sheets, that I didn't notice Alex standing in front of my locker until I nearly bumped into him.

"Hey, daydreamer," he said with a smile as I pulled my head out of the clouds. "Didn't you hear me say your name? You almost walked right by."

"Sorry," I said, feeling a blush creeping across my cheeks because he'd caught me in Sawyer-adoration mode.

"Don't be. I'm glad you looked happy." He tucked his hands into his pockets, looking suddenly, surprisingly bashful. "Look, I feel bad about what happened on Saturday. I just wanted to make sure you were okay—"

"Thanks," I said, cutting him off. I didn't want to rehash it all over again, especially now that I'd gotten it off my mind. "I'm fine. Really."

He nodded, but his eyes stayed on mine, as if he wasn't entirely convinced. "So we're good, then?" he asked. "You haven't written me off as a complete pest?"

I laughed. "I haven't written you off. The jury's still out on the pest part."

"I knew it." Relief swept his face, and he elbowed me. "I told you. I have a habit of growing on people. You like me. Admit it."

It was supposed to sound joking, I was sure, but there seemed to be an earnestness underneath his smile that made my heart unwittingly speed up. I swallowed, telling myself I imagined it.

"Like who?" a familiar voice said at my shoulder. My heart somersaulted as I turned to see Sawyer watching me intently.

"No one," I blurted, then immediately backtracked. "No!

That's not true. I like someone." Omigod, what was I saying?! *"Everyone."* I blew out a breath, my face blazing. "I like everyone."

I almost didn't dare raise my eyes, but when I did, it was into Sawyer's amused face.

"Glad to hear how you feel about . . . everyone," he said, his smile growing. "I was just on my way into lunch, if you want to come—"

"Sure!" He didn't need to ask twice.

There was an awkward millisecond of silence before he added, "Alex, you can hang with us, too . . ."

"No," Alex said quickly, seeming suddenly eager to leave. "Thanks." He gave us a wave, then added to me, "I'll see you at the mall later this week?"

"Um, yeah," I said, irritation flaring inside me. Why did he have to bring the mall up in front of Sawyer, when he knew I hadn't told Sawyer about working there? It would only start questions, and sure enough, as soon as Alex was gone, Sawyer turned to me.

"The mall?" he asked.

I shrugged nonchalantly. "I was thinking about going to pick up some Cocoa Cravings hot chocolate for my big Secret Santa gift for the holiday party next week," I lied.

Sawyer nodded. "I still need to get the last gift for mine, too. I want it to be perfect."

Perfect. The word melted my heart. He wanted my last gift to be perfect.

We got to the doorway of the cafeteria, and his hand brushed against my shoulder.

"Wait a sec," he said. "I wanted to ask you something." I froze, my pulse skittering hopefully. "You know, Sweet Garbage is doing our Bah Humbug concert on Friday night at the Teen Center. And your photo sort of makes you a part of the album. Whenever I look at it, I can see how much my music inspired it."

"You can?" I asked, surprised. That wasn't exactly how the photo had happened, but I didn't want to burst his bubble. "I mean, it did!"

He nodded knowingly. "You and Jez should come Friday."

Hope surged through me. I heard myself say, "I'd love to come."

He smiled, wide and full. "Cool." Then, when I thought my knees would buckle if he looked at me for even a second longer, he swiveled on his heel and loped into the cafeteria.

As I walked in beside him, I saw Jez, Gabe, and a few of the other Undergrounds take notice. It could've been my imagination, but I thought I glimpsed understanding on their faces, as if they were accepting some new element into their midst. As if Sawyer and I weren't just walking in together. We *were* together.

"Like a couple," Nyssa cried delightedly when I found her waiting at my locker after lunch. "That's how you and Sawyer looked when you walked into the caf." She pulled a compact from her purse to check her makeup. "I just stopped by your locker to share that."

I grinned. "Thanks. I didn't think you even knew where my locker was."

"Oh, I knew, but honestly," she said, peering inside it, her nose crinkling, "you should really consider some accessorizing."

"My coffin pencil case is as far as I'll go," I said drily. "Sorry."

She clucked her tongue. "That's just morbid." Then she smiled. "So you two are meshing, just like I predicted?"

"He invited me to his concert Friday," I told her as we walked to our classes. "But we'll see what happens. It's not like he was asking me on a date or anything."

"He will," Nyssa said with confidence. "I wonder if he'll ask you out after the holiday party next week. You know, when he tells you he's your Secret Santa. That would be like a Hallmark commercial." She sighed. "They always make me cry."

"I hate Hallmark," I said, rolling my eyes at her starry-eyed smile.

"Of course you'd hate them. But they sort of make me wish for the kind of close-knit family I don't have." She shrugged. "Anyway, what are you going to wear to the concert? Please tell me it won't be black."

I raised an eyebrow. "You don't know me enough to give me fashion advice."

She pursed her lips, "Excuse me, but when you set the fashion standards for the entire school, you can give advice to anyone you want." I laughed at that, but her expression remained undaunted. Wow, she actually believed it! "I could loan you something," she continued. "I have a coral cardigan that would look adorable on you."

"Cardigan? Adorable?" My eyes widened in horror. "Those words are banned from my vocab."

She sighed. "Fine, but don't say I didn't try . . ."

"I appreciate the offer," I said more gently, seeing how sincere she looked.

I reached into my bag to make sure I had the books I needed for my next class, then froze as my hand hit something foreign and crinkly. I pulled out a round, heavy object wrapped in silver tissue paper. A note dangled from it that read: *Here's a little something from across the universe. Your Secret Santa.*

"Ooh. Gift number three's arrived!" Nyssa said, her eyes lighting up. "Open it!"

Her enthusiasm was contagious. I ripped it open, then gasped as the tissue fell away to reveal a Beatles snow globe with a tiny yellow submarine suspended inside. It was made from a mason jar and a plastic bathtub toy, with a photo of the Beatles pasted inside. It had to be one of the most creative ideas I'd ever seen.

"This is fantastic!" I cried, giving it a shake to watch tiny strawberry-shaped confetti rain down around the submarine. "And I was talking with Sawyer about the Beatles last Friday during lunch! We're definitely on the same wavelength."

"Yeah," Nyssa said, suddenly avoiding my eyes. "Um, listen, Em. I totally think you and Sawyer are peas in an Underground pod. But hypothetically speaking, the Secret Santa thing may not be exactly what it seems . . ."

My brow crinkled. "What do you mean?"

She shook her head. "Nothing. I can't believe I almost gave it away."

"Gave what away?"

But she was already hurrying down the hall. "Never mind. It's all good!" She was rambling. "The concert will be great. See you later!"

I stared after her, baffled. What had that been all about? I didn't have a clue. But I decided it didn't matter. I couldn't expect to understand Nyssa, even if I was starting to like her.

A contented warmth filled me as I turned down the hall to my class. One thing was for sure. My day might have gotten off to a rocky start, but nothing was going to ruin the rest of it.

Or that's what I thought until three hours later, at Cocoa Cravings, when I told Alex that Sawyer had invited me to the concert.

"The concert, huh?" Alex mumbled. "I guess you're pretty excited about that."

"You *guess*?" I repeated in disbelief. "Of course I am! This is huge for me."

"Just . . . don't get your hopes up too high." His eyes flicked to my face for a second, then shifted right back to the floor. "Maybe he only wants another groupie."

"Hey, I'm no groupie," I snapped, shifting my feet uncomfortably.

"All I was trying to say is . . ." He sighed, shaking his head. "Look, let's drop the whole thing, okay?"

"No," I persisted. "You have something to say, so say it."

"Fine." He propped the mop against the wall and ducked behind the counter to clean the hot chocolate machines. "I think you have Sawyer on a pedestal. You've spent so much time creating this perfect idea of him in your head, you're not seeing everything realistically."

"That's so typical," I grumbled, frowning at him. "Instead of letting me enjoy this, you have to push my buttons."

"Oh, and you don't push mine? I told you we should drop it, but you don't know when to quit."

I threw up my hands and turned to leave. "I don't know why I even told you!"

I had one foot out the door when Alex called out, "Em, wait!"

I froze, torn between my urge to keep walking and my reluctance to leave angry. Sure, we were always debating each other, and if I was honest, I enjoyed the challenge of it, even looking forward to our joking squabbles. This felt different, though, like he had this pent-up annoyance at me that I was only registering for the first time. I didn't know where it was coming from, or why. But I didn't want to end things on a sour note. It didn't feel right. Not with Alex.

I turned with a huff. "What?"

His smile was slow to come, but I was relieved to see it when it did. "I haven't given you your hot chocolate yet." His voice was straining toward playfulness, but it fell short.

I gave a clipped laugh, then walked slowly back to the counter. "You're never going to give up, are you?"

"On you? Not a chance." He set a steaming cup on the counter and nodded. "Go on. I call this one Peppermint Patty."

I couldn't help but grin over the steaming cup, then took a sip. "Hmmm," I said, tapping my chin thoughtfully and shifting into a snobbish British accent. "The minty undertones are refreshing, leaving a chill on the tongue. They strike a nice balance with the chocolate."

Alex's face lightened hopefully. "No way. Could it be that I conquered the Master Cocoa Critic?"

I made a big show of seeming to debate. "Mmmmm . . . no." I grinned as his head dropped in melodramatic defeat. "But, I have to admit, you're getting closer."

"I knew it!" he cried triumphantly. "All I need is a little more time to perfect my formula." He rubbed his hands together in mad-scientist fashion. Then we were both laughing, and the awkward tension I'd felt between us vanished. When our laughter died down, Alex's expression softened, the indifference from earlier gone.

"Sorry about before," he said quietly. "That all came out wrong. I wasn't trying to pick a fight." His eyes were thoughtful, and full of the kindheartedness that had become so familiar to me over the last few weeks. "You shouldn't come to me for advice about Sawyer. I'm not any good at crushes."

"Does that mean you have one?" I asked, feeling a sudden and inexplicable sinking in my stomach.

"No," he blurted, staring at the floor. "A while ago, there was a girl I'd thought maybe . . ." He shook his head, but I caught his creeping blush before he ducked his head behind the counter to straighten the toppings containers. "But it was never going to happen. She had her heart set on somebody else."

"Oh." I felt a wave of relief. I'd never imagined Alex crushing on a girl before, and the idea made me feel unsettled and strangely jealous. But I couldn't be jealous! That was impossible. I'd be happy for him if he found a girlfriend. Wouldn't I? "Well, Sawyer might not happen, either. I'm only going to the concert." I tried to sound as casual as possible, but my heart raced at the thought.

Alex nodded. "Anyway, there's something I've been meaning to tell you."

"What's that?"

He gestured at my elf costume. "Your outfit. It's missing something . . ."

"Really?" I said hopefully. "If my ears fell off, good riddance! I hope I never see them again!"

He shook his head. "No . . . something else." He pulled a container of whipped cream from behind his back and aimed it at me. "Snow!" Before I had time to react, he squirted the whipped cream toward my face. The can was nearly empty, which made the stream of white spray out in a volcanic spritz.

I screeched, then leapt behind the counter and tackled him. "Oh, you are *so* going to pay for that." I wrestled the can from his hands, aimed, and fired, and white flecks splayed across his face. He tickled me to loosen my grasp on the can, but I depressed the nozzle, and soon, we were both covered in white.

We were bent over laughing and nearly out of breath when I heard someone clear his throat. We glanced up into the astonished face of Alex's *abuelo*.

"¿*Qué pasó?*" he asked, surveying the dusting of white coating most of the counter, floor, and us. But there was a smile on his face. "The whipped cream has been misbehaving again, eh?"

I snuffled a giggle, and Alex and I began brushing at the whipped cream sprinkled all over our clothes.

"*Lo siento*, Abuelo," Alex said, his voice light with laughter. "Sorry. We'll clean up everything."

"*No te preocupes*," Señor Perez said with a dismissive wave before heading toward the shop's back room. "Fun is always worth a little mess."

As the back room door swung shut, I caught Alex's eye, and we cracked up all over again. But as we finished cleaning and closing up the store together, I felt a niggling in my stomach. I couldn't help wondering, What would Sawyer have done if he'd been with us in Cocoa Cravings tonight? Would he have been hiding behind the counter with me, laughing ridiculously and ducking sprays of whipped cream?

I tried to imagine him there beside me, but somehow, the picture never quite crystallized in my mind.

Chapter Eight

"Are you sure this dress looks okay?" I asked Jez for the hundredth time as the car pulled up in front of the Teen Center.

"It looks just like it did two minutes ago. *And* two minutes before that." She gave me a teasing look as she patted down the layers of her glittery pink tutu. "Fabulous."

I smiled gratefully. "Thanks." But I still couldn't stop smoothing the layers of purple lace that made up the skirt.

I'd chosen my favorite dress for the concert—it had a fitted black sleeveless bodice adorned with zippers. I paired it with black leggings, a purple feathered barrette in my hair, and my Doc Marten boots. (I was sure Nyssa would be horrified, which was how I knew it was perfect.) It was an outfit I always felt great in, but tonight, it wasn't doing a thing to settle my nerves.

Jez's mom leaned over the front seat, peering at us sternly. "All right, Emery, Jasmina." Beside me, I felt Jez stiffen at the use of her full name. Her mom refused to call her by her nickname, and it was a constant source of frustration for Jez. "Mr. Mason will pick you up at ten."

"Come on, Em." Jez swung the door open. "Let's go find the boys—I mean—band."

"What?!" Mrs. Vesudez cried, but Jez was already shutting the door, laughing.

I shook my head at her. "You keep messing with her head, and she'll never let you out of the house."

"Sure she will." Jez slipped her arm through mine. "She thinks you're a good influence on me." I snorted, and she grinned.

Then I took a deep breath. "Let's do it."

We walked into the Teen Center, where a disco ball threw beads of light in spinning rivers around the darkened room.

Groups of kids, most of whom I recognized from school, mingled on the floor and around a snack table set up toward the back. My breath caught when I spotted Sawyer talking with Gabe and a few other Undergrounds at the front of the room by the stage.

He looked adorable in his faded, ripped jeans and a black hoodie with a vintage Blink-182 tee over top. *See me, see me, see me*, I thought, pounding out a hopeful rhythm in my heart. Finally, he lifted his head and our eyes met. He stopped talking midsentence, then smiled, and my knees turned to putty as he headed in our direction.

"Hey," he said when he reached me. "I'm glad you made it."

He was? He was! I blinked in blissful delirium but couldn't find my voice until Jez squeezed my arm. "Me too!" I finally spluttered. I motioned around the room. "It looks like a great turnout. Are you nervous about performing in front of so many people?"

A flicker of amusement lit his face. "Nah. I have this mindfulness thing I do. I pick one person in the audience and imagine I'm playing just for them." He shrugged. "It makes it easier. Besides, my music has a deeper meaning. I can't let something as pedestrian as stage fright stand in its way."

Pedestrian. How much did I love that he used words like that? "It's cool that you can do that. You know, visualize."

"Sawyer!" A voice called, and we looked toward the stage to see Gabe waving him over. "It's time to warm up."

"That's my cue," he said. "I've got to get backstage."

Sigh. The casual way he threw "backstage" out there made him sound like such a bona fide pro.

"I've always wondered what goes on back there," I said to him. "Top secret rituals? Signing autographs? Bingeing on gummy worms and Pixy Stix?"

I expected him to laugh at the joke, but his expression stayed serious. "It's all about focusing, you know, getting in the right place mentally."

"Oh," I said, suddenly feeling foolish for making a joke, when clearly Sawyer took pre-concert prepping pretty seriously. I also felt a little disappointed that it wasn't anything more exciting. "I'd love to check it out sometime," I said, hinting.

I'd hoped he'd jump on that, but his brow furrowed. "Yeah, the thing is, normally, I need my space after a show. To decompress, you know."

Omigod, this was embarrassing. I'd put myself out there, and now he was rejecting me. "Of course!" I blurted, smiling to let him know I was totally okay with that. "It's fine. I didn't really—"

"No, I'm sorry. You can come backstage afterward." He put his hand on mine, and I trembled at his touch. "I can unwind later."

"Are you sure?" I asked, and he nodded.

"And hey," he added, "I saved you and Jez some seats in the front row for the show."

"Really?" I asked, then mentally kicked myself for sounding so thrilled. "Thanks. That was nice of you."

"Well, I had some ulterior motives." He looked at me from under that fringe of jagged bangs. "I want to see you while I sing." My entire body liquefied at his words, and I was grateful the darkness hid my blush.

Jez nodded enthusiastically. "We'll be the best groupies you've ever had."

At "groupies," his brow crinkled ever so slightly. "That sounds way too Justin Bieber for Sweet Garbage."

"Definitely!" I laughed, commiserating, then rolled my eyes at Jez.

She glanced at me questioningly, then caught on and jumped in with "Right! Who needs legions of swooning, screaming fans anyway?"

Sawyer gave a short laugh. "Exactly. It's all about the music." Then he turned toward the stage, lifting a hand in parting. "See you after."

"After," I called to him jubilantly.

Jez and I hurried to grab our seats, which were—as promised—front and center. A few minutes later, the edgy, opening chords of "Hallmark Holidaze" rang out, and the stage curtain opened to reveal Sawyer at the microphone, singing in that sullen voice I adored. The bright stage lights haloed Sawyer's hair with gold, and he performed with a relaxed confidence that made him look even cuter, if that was possible.

"Wow," Jez whispered to me at one point as I snapped photos with fiendish speed, "he looks like he's in pain when he sings."

I nodded. The more I listened, the more validated I felt about my own anti-Christmas campaign. Finally, here was someone who understood exactly how I felt about the holidays! It was hard to tell with the bright lights shining on his face, but I could've sworn Sawyer kept looking at me as he sang. Then, suddenly, I didn't have to guess anymore, because as one of the songs finished, Sawyer took the microphone off the stand and sat down on the edge of the stage, right in front of me!

In the expectant silence of the room, he said, "Now, this next song is one that none of you have heard before. I wrote it a few days ago, for someone who's in the audience tonight."

I gripped the edge of my seat, my heart thrashing wildly. He couldn't mean—

He gave me an encouraging smile. "Em, could you come up here, please?"

Jez gave me a nudge. "Go on," she whispered. "Get up there."

On shaking legs, I walked to the edge of the stage and sat down beside Sawyer. Even though the gym was a sea of darkness, I sensed the dozens of eyes watching us, waiting.

"This song's called 'Winter Girl,'" Sawyer said.

Behind us onstage, Gabe struck some slow chords on his guitar, the sort of beat you'd hear in a—gulp—love song. Sawyer turned to me, put the microphone to his lips, and began to sing. The song was about a girl made of snow, one who spends her days looking out at the wintry world, making pictures in her mind. The words were beautiful, but I could barely hear them over my deafening heartbeat.

When the last note of the song faded into the darkness, applause broke out around the room, and Sawyer slipped his hand behind my back to help me slide off the stage.

I collapsed into my chair, ecstatic and breathless. At that moment, there was one thing I knew beyond any doubt. The most surefire way to get a girl to fall head over heels? Write a song for her.

I was still in a heady state of bliss when the concert ended. Jez waited at the snack table as I climbed the stairs to the stage alone and walked into the wings. I found Sawyer bent over a bunch of amps and wires, putting equipment away. I took a deep, nervous breath, wondering how things would be between us after what had happened during the concert.

I took a step toward him, and my heart skipped a beat when he glanced up and smiled.

"Hey." He motioned to a folding chair next to his, and I sat down.

"The concert was incredible," I started. "And that song." I smiled, letting my hair fall into my face. "Thank you."

"I thought you'd like it." He tucked his hair behind his ear. "I actually had the idea over a year ago. After a bad breakup with some girl who went to Garber Middle School. Can't remember her name."

"Oh," I said as brightly as I could, even as my insides deflated.

This Winter Girl wasn't me? She was some girl he couldn't even remember?

Ouch.

"Anyway," he continued, "the song wasn't coming together for me yet, until I saw those photos you took. All those icicles and snow-covered trees. The sheer desolation of winter, you know, its loneliness. Then everything solidified."

"Well, I'm glad I could help." I tried to swallow the lump in my throat. At least my photos had motivated him, but it would have been way more romantic to hear that *I'd* inspired him instead of my pictures.

"Yeah, well, I don't expect you to really understand the mystique of songwriting. But it's sweet that you're trying."

I frowned, and for a second I thought he was about to say more, but then a wave of deafening giggles crashed over us from stage right. I turned to see a dozen girls rapidly approaching, clutching CDs in their hands.

I waited as he signed CDs and chatted with the other girls, knowing that this was part of what soon-to-be-discovered artists did. Once it was all over and they'd gone, Sawyer glanced up and caught my eye, and a flicker of surprise crossed his face, as if he'd forgotten about me entirely.

"I wasn't expecting that," he said. "Fans can get so needy."

I smiled. "They really loved you."

He nodded, and then we settled into silence. He seemed completely comfortable with it, but for some reason, it made me feel awkward, and I scrambled to fill it. After all the times I'd run through imaginary conversations with Sawyer in my head, I couldn't come up with anything else to say to him now that we were finally alone? That was ridiculous! I'd always imagined us talking for hours without any effort at all.

"So, what'd you get from your Secret Santa this week?" I blurted.

He reached into his messenger bag and pulled out the composition sheets Nyssa and I had made. "Cool, right?"

"Definitely," I said. "Do you have any idea who it is?"

He shook his head. "At first, I thought it might be Nyssa. I mean, who else in our class would come up with a fruit-and-cheese gift basket? I was sure her parents probably bought it for her so she wouldn't have to go to any trouble making something herself."

I blushed for Nyssa's sake, remembering how she'd basically told me the exact same thing.

"But after the gift I got this week, I have no idea who it is," Sawyer continued. "There's no way Nyssa would've made these sheets by hand. Not the Glee Princess."

I flinched at the nickname. It was one thing to hear Nyssa poke fun at it good-naturedly herself. It was another thing to hear it spoken like an insult.

"You never know," I said lightly, trying in the gentlest way possible to help him give her the benefit of the doubt. "People might surprise you."

He paused over the wires he was holding. "Not people like her. They don't know how to think outside the box." He locked eyes with me. "You know what she's like, with her high-end fashion and attitude."

"She's not only about that," I started, my stomach pinching. I couldn't let his comments about Nyssa go without saying anything. "I used to think Nyssa was a snob, too, but I've hung out with her a little lately, and she's more down-to-earth than I ever gave her credit for."

He shook his head. "That seems hard to believe. Anyway, I don't waste a lot of time on all the Secret Santa drama. I wish I could have opted out of the whole thing."

That's exactly what I would've said a couple weeks ago, too. But it was disappointing to hear him say it now, knowing that he was my Secret Santa. Did he still find it that much of a drag, even when it was me he was giving gifts to? The idea made my insides droop. Even so, I was eager to show him that we were kindred spirits in that respect.

"I hated the idea at first, too," I admitted. "But at least it will be over next week." I said it with as much zeal as I could muster, even though I felt an unpleasant nagging sensation as I did, like I was caught in a lie.

"You read my mind." He looked at me thoughtfully, then stepped closer. "There is one thing about this holiday season I'm glad for."

"What's that?" I asked weakly, barely able to focus being so close to him.

He smiled. "It's giving me the chance to get to know you."

My heart stopped. "How?" I managed to whisper, wondering if he was about to confess that I was his Secret Santa secret.

"Well, if the band hadn't been putting together the *Bah Humbug* album, then I never would've used your photo, and maybe we wouldn't be here now. Twists of fate, you know?"

"Yeah," I breathed. He was talking about fate. *Our* fate.

"Before the last few weeks, I had you all wrong."

"What do you mean?"

He laughed. "I used to think you were Christmas-crazed, like the rest of your family. Because of the Holly Jolly House and everything."

I groaned. "Tell me about it." He laughed. "I can't stand my parents' decorations. All those tacky plastic elves and reindeer. It's completely embarrassing. Pathetic even."

I expected Sawyer to nod in agreement, but instead, his gaze shifted to something over my shoulder. Much to my disappointment, he took a slight step back from me. It was only when he said, "Hi, Mr. Mason," that I understood why.

Dad. Here. Behind me. Crud.

I turned slowly and saw Dad standing a few feet away, his expression crestfallen. That was when I realized he'd heard every single word I'd just said.

"'Pathetic,'" Dad repeated as soon as Jez shut the car door and hurried inside her house. She'd shot me a look of sympathy as she got out, since I'd managed to whisper a rundown of what had happened to her as we left the Teen Center.

"You called the Holly Jolly House 'pathetic,'" he said again, shaking his head in disbelief.

I sighed at the woeful way he spoke the word, like I'd said the worst thing imaginable. I hugged my arms against the sudden chill I felt settling over the car, turning toward the window so I wouldn't have to see Dad's downcast face.

"Dad, the Holly Jolly House is *your* thing. Not mine. I thought you knew how I felt."

"I had no idea," Dad said shortly. He pulled into our driveway, where the blaze of twinkling lights in the front yard made the inside of the car as bright as day. He turned off the ignition but didn't move to get out. "It's true, you haven't been as enthusiastic about it this year, but I kept hoping it was some phase you were going through."

I huffed, tightening my shoulders. "It's not a phase!" I cried in frustration. "This is who I am!"

Silence stretched between us as Dad stared out at the lawn, where the lit-up penguins were doing their caroling act to "Deck the Halls." When he finally spoke again, his voice was tired and wavering, almost old-sounding.

"When you were a little girl, you couldn't wait for Christmas to come." He smiled sadly. "You were the reason we started the Holly Jolly House in the first place. Me and your grandma. She told me she hoped you'd never lose your sense of wonder, and that the Holly Jolly House would help you remember—"

"Things are different than they used to be!" I cried, fighting the sudden urge I had to cover my ears with my hands. I didn't want to think about Grandma. Not tonight. "*I'm* different!"

"I see that now," Dad said, nodding slowly. He frowned over the steering wheel, as if debating, then reached into the pocket of his jacket. "Look, there's something I've been wanting to give you. I've been carrying it around with me for weeks." He set a worn red velvet jewelry box in my hands. "Grandma asked me to save this for you. You've never asked about it, and you might have forgotten, but it's her Christmas locket. She was sure you'd change your mind someday and want it. She said I'd know when the time was right." He sighed. "This may not be the perfect time, but I'm hoping this might change the way you feel."

I stared at the box, fingers trembling. I felt the weight of it in my hands, the weight of what was inside. "It won't change anything," I whispered.

Dad nodded. "I'm sorry to hear that. I didn't think you'd ever get too old for Christmas. Your mom and I haven't. Your Grandma never did, either. But I guess . . ." He sighed. "I guess we were wrong about you."

My heart sank as he got out of the car and walked inside, leaving me alone. I blinked fiercely, my eyes stinging with tears I wouldn't let fall.

I hadn't meant to hurt Dad. Couldn't he even try to understand my point of view?

I glanced toward the house and, through one of the front windows, caught a glimpse of Mom and Dad talking in the kitchen. My stomach tensed. No way was I going inside with them in the kitchen. I didn't want to talk anymore tonight.

I sat back in my seat to wait for them to head upstairs and reached into my bag for the photo of me and Grandma. There she was, her arms snug around me, smiling beautifully. I shoved the jewelry box into my coat pocket. I didn't want to imagine what Grandma would've thought if she'd heard me tonight. I knew the answer. I could feel her disappointment even in her absence, and it stayed with me through the rest of the long, sleepless night that followed.

Chapter Nine

I avoided going downstairs as long as possible the next morning, but by ten o'clock, my growling stomach couldn't hold out anymore. Plus, I knew Mom would be pounding on my door soon enough to get me out of bed to go to work at the mall, so there was no point delaying the inevitable.

I grabbed my elf outfit, which much to my vexation, Mom had salvaged so not a single trace of my whipped cream battle with Alex remained. Then I headed for the kitchen, where I found Mom with her laptop going through photo proofs. The second her eyes met mine with that "how could you?" glare, my chest tightened, and my lips felt dangerously close to quivering. Ugh!! She was an expert at the guilt trip, no doubt about it.

"Your plate's in the microwave," she said tersely. "Your dad's getting dressed. He'll be down in a minute. We have to leave in fifteen minutes to open the Wonderland."

I nodded, focusing on the microwave's buttons to avoid looking at her.

She snapped her laptop shut, heaving a sigh. "Honestly, Em, I don't know what's gotten into you lately. Your dad's been sulking around here all morning. How could you say something like that about our house?"

"I didn't know he was listening," I protested, sitting down and pushing my eggs around my plate. "Besides, it's not the end of the world."

"No, you're right about that." Mom stood to pour the last bit of her coffee down the drain. "But couldn't you at least humor him?"

I threw up my hands. "I was only being honest, Mom. Since when is that a criminal offense?"

"It's not," Dad said, walking into the kitchen in his Santa

suspenders, his pillow-stuffed belly protruding lumpily from his white shirt. He gave me a quick peck on the forehead, which I took with relief as a peacemaking gesture. "Of course we want you to have your own opinions, and we'll do our best to respect them." He slipped on his giant red coat. "Which is why I've decided this will be the last year for the Holly Jolly House."

My stomach plunged, and Mom gaped. "What?" she breathed.

Dad nodded in an attempt to look casually unaffected. Still, the light in his eyes dimmed. "It's time," he said simply. "It's getting to be too much work." He glanced at my mom. "You know what it does to my back. I threw it out once already, putting all the decorations up."

"Dad," I started. "You don't have to—"

"I do." He cleared his throat, slid on his Santa beard, put on a jolly face, and clapped his hands together. "Time to go, isn't it? We don't want to be late!"

With that, he disappeared into the garage to start the car.

"Wow," I said. I used to imagine that if this ever happened, I'd be so relieved. But all I felt was sickening guilt. "Do you think he's okay?"

"I don't know. I'm so used to seeing him light up like a toddler every Christmas. This is completely new to me." Mom turned toward the sink, shaking her head and staring out the window. "It's the end of an era," she said quietly. She glanced at me, bewildered. "It's silly, but I feel like crying."

I didn't answer, but it was the strangest thing. So did I.

My guilt only got worse as the day wore on. Dad did his same old Santa routine at the North Pole Wonderland, but when he needed my help with posing kids for photos or printing out receipts, he didn't make any cheesy Christmas puns, like he usually did, or tug on my elf hat in attempts to get me to smile. He was careful to avoid doing anything I normally would've griped about.

Dad's stilted politeness became so awkward that when he asked me if I'd walk over to Cocoa Cravings to see if Señor Perez had some hot chocolate trays ready to bring over, I jumped at the chance to escape.

When I saw Alex wave from behind the counter, I hesitated. I wanted to tell him everything that had happened last night, but I worried about what he'd say when he heard about my dad.

"Hey, you," he said when I got to the counter. "Abuelo's getting some trays ready in the back, but it will be a few minutes. Enough time for you to try this." He set a cup of hot chocolate on the counter for me. "It's Licorice Love."

"I do love licorice, but with chocolate? I have my doubts." I took a sip, then shook my head. "Weird combo. Ick."

"Abuelo said the same thing. I thought I'd give it a shot anyway." He dumped the rest into the sink behind the counter, frowning.

"You're upset. Great." I sighed. "I can add your name to the list of people mad at me."

"Sorry." He studied the counter. "It's not you. I'm just not having a great weekend. Sounds like you didn't, either?"

"Well, Sawyer's concert was great." Alex nodded, but even as he did, a line appeared between his eyebrows, like he was still irritated. "I took a load of pictures. Want to see?"

"Actually, maybe another time," he said, turning away. "I'm pretty busy today—"

"Funny," I snorted. "There's not a customer in sight. Come on!

It'll only take a sec." I took his silence as agreement and pulled my camera out of my bag, but when I tried the view function, nothing happened. "I can't believe it." I rubbed my forehead in frustration. "It's dead." I slid it back into my bag. "It's *so* time for a new camera. I just hope I don't lose all those photos. I had some great ones of Sawyer." I blushed, remembering the thrill I'd gotten being so close to him last night. "He wrote a song for me, and brought me up onstage to sing it to me."

Alex rolled his eyes. "A personal serenade?" He fiddled with some knobs on one of the hot chocolate machines. "Of course. What girl wouldn't fall for that?" He smiled, but it didn't reach his eyes. "Did you faint away in his arms, too?"

"No," I said defensively, staring at him. "Look, I don't know what you have against Sawyer, but can you not ruin this for me? Please? My day's off to a rough enough start to begin with."

Alex looked at me for a long minute, then nodded. "Fine." But his tone was tinged with grudging. "So, why's your day so bad?"

I grimaced. "There was this completely awkward thing that happened with my dad that I feel horrible about, and Sawyer was there. It wasn't the way I'd imagined the night ending."

"How did you imagine it ending?" Alex asked quietly, his voice edged with irritation. "With Sawyer kissing you?"

I glared at him, hating his tone. Why did it seem like he was so intent on picking fights today? "No! I don't know. Maybe." I bit my lip. "I mean, I would've liked it if he had. But obviously you don't approve, or whatever."

He shook his head. "You don't get it. You never will."

I threw up my hands. "Get what? I feel like I'm trying to guess the sphinx's riddle here. Just spell it out for me, why don't you!"

"Let's not talk about it anymore, all right?" His jaw tightened, and I could tell he was holding something back. He was angry but trying not to let it show. "Just tell me what happened with your dad."

I took a deep breath and told him everything. I was afraid to look at him as I talked, worried that if I did, I'd see the same disappointment I'd seen on my parents' faces. I didn't think I could take it from him, too. But when I finished the story, he only nodded sympathetically.

"That's pretty awful," he said. "Especially since there's no easy way to make it right. You already apologized, so now I guess you wait for it to blow over."

"If it ever does," I said forlornly. "I never meant for my dad to hear me."

"I know. Maybe you were trying so hard to impress Sawyer that you said something that wasn't really true."

"Of course it was true!" I blurted. "The Holly Jolly House *is* embarrassing! I just never planned to say that out loud in front of Dad." Alex nodded, but his expression was doubtful. "You don't believe me!"

"You're right. I don't."

My mouth dropped open, but he only shrugged. "You're trying to convince yourself that you're someone you're not."

"How can you say that?" I slid off the stool and started pacing. "I shouldn't have told you. I *knew* that the second I told you, you were going to shift into high-and-mighty mode." I glared at him. "You'll never understand me. Not the way Sawyer does."

Alex frowned. "Oh, sure. You think Sawyer knows you so well." His eyes glinted with anger. "Have you even told him the truth?"

"About how much I hate the holidays? You know I have."

He shook his head. "No. Have you told him that you're working as an elf at the North Pole Wonderland? Or have you conveniently forgotten that part of who you are?"

"That's not who I am!" I cried. "That's what my parents are making me do!"

"What about your grandma?" he asked quietly. "Have you told him about her?"

I jerked back. "Why would I?"

"Because she's the reason why you still love Christmas," he said. "Deep down inside, even though you won't admit it."

I swallowed hard, the weight of everything that had happened in the last twenty-four hours crashing down on me.

"I don't have to listen to this." I turned toward the door. "Honestly, I don't even know why I ever thought we could get along. We're too different."

"This has nothing to do with our differences," Alex said. "This has to do with being honest with yourself. About everything. Your grandma, Sawyer, and—" He stopped suddenly, flustered, and I wondered what else he'd been about to say.

"Forget it," I said flatly. "I thought we could be friends. But we can't. Not anymore."

The stricken look on his face made me drop my eyes, and instantly, remorse coursed through me. But too much had been said already. So I turned on my heel and walked away without another word.

When the phone rang later that night and Mom called up the stairs that it was for me, I felt instant relief. It was him, I knew it was. Everything was going to be okay.

"I'm so glad you called!" I blurted as soon as I put the phone to my ear.

"I knew you would be," that familiar, smooth voice responded.

"Sawyer?" I asked.

He laughed lightly. "Who else would it be?"

My heart somersaulted, torn between disappointment and excitement. I was so sure it had been Alex calling. I'd picked up the phone at least a dozen times over the last hour, fingers hovering over the digits ready to dial, wanting to make things right.

Then I'd argue myself out of it, telling myself that this was all his doing and he should be the one to apologize to me.

"Em, are you there?" Sawyer asked.

I hit my mental "reset" button now, focusing on the fact that Sawyer was on the other end of the line. "Yeah, I'm here!" I said brightly. "How's your weekend going?"

"Great, actually. I spent all morning composing. I need a sounding board, and I thought maybe I could sing a few lines for you."

I grinned. Sawyer wanted my advice on his music! "Sure! I'd love to hear what you've got."

"Great." And without saying another word, he began singing. I lay back on my bed, marveling at the poetry he'd strung together and at the fact that, right now, I was the only person in the whole world that he was performing for.

"So what do you think?" he asked after a few minutes.

"Wow," I breathed. "You're onto something for sure. I mean, there were a couple lines that were a little clunky, like the 'lies like the flies buzzing around the cans of calamity.' But if you smooth them out, then—"

"Clunky?" He sounded annoyed.

"Oh, sorry, I didn't mean 'clunky' as in awful. Maybe it needs a tiny bit more work is all."

Silence filled the phone, and then finally he said, "I'll run it by Gabe. He's got more of an ear and gets what I'm aiming for. It's tough to understand the themes if you're not musical."

"What?" I stiffened. "I love music—"

"I know you do," he interrupted. "Only, you consume it, you don't create it. That's a huge difference."

I sat up in bed, rankled and wanting to defend myself. "Yeah, but I understand art. I create photos."

He laughed. "Not the same thing, Em. Not even close. But, hey, thanks for giving it a listen anyway."

"Sure," I said, spirits sinking.

"So, how's your weekend?" he asked.

"I've had better," I said, then waited for him to ask what was wrong so I could tell him what had happened with my dad and Alex.

Instead, though, Sawyer mumbled distractedly into the phone,

"Great. That's great. Well, I should probably sign off." His voice sounded more distant, like maybe he'd set the phone down, and I could hear rustlings of paper in the background like he was packing up his stuff.

"Oh. Okay." My voice sounded small and disappointed. This was not the way I'd imagined my first phone call with Sawyer going at all. Sure, the singing had been romantic, at first, but having a more satisfying talk would have been better. "I'll talk to you later?"

"Sure thing." There was a click.

I flopped against my pillows in frustration. First Dad, then Alex, and now Sawyer. I felt like I was missing the mark with everyone lately.

The voice came from a distance, and I struggled to pull myself out of my haze to focus.

"Emmmmm," it called. "Earth to Em!"

"Sorry," I said, blinking an exasperated-looking Nyssa into focus.

"I was saying, how about this one?" She studied the shelves of nail polish along the wall of the salon, then held up a pastel pink polish. "Flamingo Flambé?"

I snorted. "I object on principle alone." I scrutinized the color. "And it's too bright."

"Ugh." Nyssa jutted out her hip, glaring at me. "You're absolutely no help at all. I don't even know why I asked you to meet me here."

"That makes two of us," I quipped. Nyssa's phone call had come early this morning, and when she'd asked me to meet her at Sassy Nail Salon, I'd nearly choked on my cereal. "So," I said to her now, "what am I doing here, *really*?"

"I told you. I wanted you to help me brainstorm ideas for Sawyer's last Secret Santa gift."

"We could've done that over the phone," I pointed out. In fact, it had just taken us about a minute to decide on Sawyer's final gift. I'd come up with the brainstorm after the concert on Friday, and Nyssa loved it. She was going to talk to her dad about setting up a private tour for Sawyer at her dad's recording studio. It would be perfect.

"Well, I also needed your help picking out a nail color for the glee show tonight," Nyssa said offhandedly, not wanting to meet my eyes.

"Nyssa. You want *my* advice on nail polish?" I raised my eyebrows. "You're clearly desperate. Come clean. Now."

She stomped her foot in this hilariously childish manner. "Fine. I asked you to come with me because none of my other friends would. My parents are leaving for a trip to London in two hours, and Dana and the rest of the glee peeps all made afternoon appointments for their manis." She shrugged. "I thought it would be fun to have some company."

We sat down at a nail station with her color of choice, Beautiful Blush.

"To be honest," Nyssa continued as the manicurist filed her nails, "I can't believe you actually agreed to come with me. I'm glad, but . . . why did you, anyway?"

I sighed. "My house is like a minefield of awkwardness right now."

"Sounds juicy." She grinned. "I'm all ears."

I laughed, in spite of myself, and then gave her the details of what had happened over the weekend with my dad and then with Alex. When I'd finished talking, she fixed her Barbie-blue eyes on me.

"I have solutions to all of your problems," she said matter-of-factly, waving her newly polished nails in the air to dry them.

I laughed. "These I've *got* to hear."

"First, apologize to Alex."

"There's no way I'm apologizing to him." Yes, I'd had that brief moment of weakness last night when I'd thought it was Alex calling. But Alex's opinion shouldn't matter to me. It *wouldn't*. "He drives me crazy!" I said. "And if he thinks for one second I'm going to give him the satisfaction of watching me grovel—"

"But Alex probably has his own reasons for why he's acting the way he is," Nyssa said. She glanced toward the ceiling. "Who knows what they are? But . . . he's a good guy." She gave me a pointed look. "Trust me on that."

I threw up my hands. "Oh, sure, now you're an authority on Alex *and* fashion?"

She blinked innocently. "I'm talented, what can I say?" I

laughed, and then her face got serious. "And as far as your dad goes," she said. "Maybe cut him a little slack. Your parents sound great, even with the Christmas obsession. And at least they're around. They *want* to be a part of your life." She bit her lip. "Mine are away so much. They miss out on a lot."

I froze, mentally slapping my forehead as I put two and two together. How had I not realized this before? "Your parents aren't going to your concert tonight, are they?"

"They'll be on the plane for London. A three-day trip." She sighed, then shook it off with a smile. "It's fine. I'm used to them missing my stuff."

"That stinks," I said, suddenly feeling embarrassed by my own attitude toward my parents. "I'm sorry."

"It's okay. Don't worry about me."

But after her nails dried and we said good-bye, what she'd said about her parents stayed with me. The thought of her singing at the glee concert without them in the audience gave me a hollow ache in my stomach. I'd been planning on giving Nyssa a small gift certificate to the A La Mode fashion jewelry boutique on

Main Street for her final Secret Santa gift. But suddenly, that didn't feel right. I wanted to give her something different. Something she'd never expect.

As Mom drove me home from the salon, I asked her if I could borrow her camera. Mine still wasn't working, and Mom had told me it might have shuttered its last frame.

"Of course, honey," she said. "But what do you need it for?"

"The glee concert tonight," I said with a smile. "I need to go, and if it's okay, I think you and dad should come, too."

Three hours later, I walked into Fairview Middle School's auditorium with my plan in place. Mom, Dad, and I took our seats. Dad and I were tiptoeing around each other, and he'd seemed surprised that I'd asked him to come along to the show at all. Still, I knew he wouldn't turn down anything involving holiday music, and Mom was sitting between us as a buffer to the awkwardness. As soon as the curtain rose, I started snapping photos. Nyssa looked beautiful up on the stage, and she gave a performance that would've put Lea Michele to shame.

After the show, Mom and Dad, who I'd told about Nyssa's

absentee parents, found Nyssa in the wings and gushed over her performance, just like I knew they would. Nyssa beamed, delighted.

"You didn't tell me you were coming," she said, elbowing me.

"Would you have believed me if I had?" I grinned.

She laughed. "Never in a million years." Then she added in a whisper, "I can see right through that Underground armor of yours, Em. I'm on to you, and . . ." She squeezed me hand. "Thank you."

I felt a glow at her words. "You're welcome."

We didn't stay long, because Nyssa's hordes of admirers and fellow glee clubbers soon surrounded her for hugs, but I felt great as we headed for home. Mom's camera was full of photos, and by nine o' clock that night, I'd proofed and printed thirty pictures of the concert. I'd pick up a nice album tomorrow after school, put the photos in it, and give it to Nyssa at the party.

I felt like it was the first thing I'd managed to get right all weekend. Still, though, it wasn't enough to make me forget about Dad. Or Alex. Not even close.

Chapter Ten

I searched the faces in the cafeteria, looking for that unmistakable curly hair, those twinkling eyes. But as students trickled into the lunch line and to the tables, there was no sign of him. I hadn't heard from him or seen him since Saturday, and now it was Wednesday. I was sure he was still mad about our fight, and so was I, but I hadn't expected it to make him drop off the face of the earth. Worry twisted my insides. Where was he?

"Looking for me, I hope?" a voice said at my shoulder, and I turned to see Sawyer smiling at me, holding his cafeteria tray in his hands.

"Hi," I said too quickly, flustered that I'd been caught off guard by his question. "Um . . . yes. You." My voice swung up enthusiastically even as my stomach sunk a notch. Of course I was happy to see him, but I knew if I didn't ask now, the question would bug me the rest of the day. "And, actually, has Alex been in history class? I haven't seen him all week."

Sawyer shook his head. "He's been sick." He motioned for me to follow him to the stage. "Come on, let's grab our spot."

My heart flipped. *Our spot.* But the giddiness only lasted a second before worry quashed it.

"Sick?" I repeated as we sat down in a spot near Jez, Gabe, and the other Undergrounds. It was a few feet away from the rest of the group, though, which made it feel more private, almost like Sawyer and I were having a lunch "date."

"He has a cold, I guess," Sawyer said casually. "I dropped off some homework for him yesterday after school."

"Oh." I nodded. Well, at least Alex didn't hate me so much that he'd left the country. At least, not yet.

Seeing him at the mall had become a habit, I'd realized in the quiet boredom of the North Pole Wonderland this week. It was also something I looked forward to. Without Alex there to harass me with hot chocolate or pick good-natured fights, my hours at the photo booth had stretched out painfully.

As Sawyer worked on songs with Gabe over lunch, I tried to stay tuned in to the music. But my mind kept drifting to Alex. I wasn't even aware of it until Sawyer nudged my elbow.

"Hey, you've been spacing all lunch. Did you hear any of my songs?"

"Sure! I was listening." But he didn't look convinced. "Sorry," I added sheepishly. "Just . . . thinking." What was wrong with me? Here I was, sitting next to my one-and-only crush, and I was stressing over Alex? Ridiculous!

Sawyer's expression turned sour. "You've been doing that a lot this week." He shrugged. "If my music's not that important to you, then—"

"No!" I protested. "It is!" A rush of blood heated my face. "Things have been a little tense at home, that's all."

He scoffed. "Don't tell me. Your dad's still miffed."

"Yeah." With the exception of the smile he'd had during Nyssa's glee concert, Dad had been in a funk all week. When it came to putting up our own Christmas tree in the family room, he did it with Mom one day after I left for school. I came home to find it twinkling in our front window. The final knife to the heart was the star tree topper. No matter how much I protested, Dad always managed to guilt me into putting it on top. "You've been doing it since you were born," he said each year. "It's bad luck to break tradition."

Not this year, though. When I walked in to find the star already glowing atop the tree, Dad offered me his new, sad smile. "I went ahead and put it up. No sense in pretending you wanted to, right?"

Now I took a halfhearted bite of my sandwich and said to Sawyer, "I guess I didn't expect my dad to take it so hard."

Sawyer nodded. "It does seem ridiculous. You were only standing up for what you believe."

My throat tightened. There was so much I'd held back from him as we'd gotten to know each other over the last couple of weeks. What would he think if he knew about my alter elf ego? He'd think I was as big of a fake as all the other "poseurs."

"I don't know," I said quietly. "Maybe I could pretend a little. For my dad's sake."

"Why would you do that?" He stared at me like I'd said something unfathomable.

I sighed. "Because I don't want to hurt his feelings. I mean, he's my *dad*."

"Yeah. But sometimes honesty comes at a price." He said it so matter-of-factly that it sounded harsh. "Your dad will get over it. And in the meantime, you should focus on something else. Negativity drags me down. It gets old fast."

I stared at him. What was he saying? That he thought I was griping too much? I swallowed anxiously, wondering if he might be getting tired of me. Then, to my relief, he put his hand on my shoulder and smiled.

"Besides, Christmas will be over by next week, and then the Holly Jolly House will be gone forever."

I nodded, adding a weak, "I can't wait."

"*I* can't wait to get the homeroom party over with tomorrow," Sawyer said with an eye roll. The party, which had originally been scheduled for Friday night, had been bumped up to Thursday because there was a snowstorm in the forecast. "I'm sure you're just as sick of Mrs. Finnegan's Secret Santa countdown as I am."

I nibbled on my fruit salad, hesitating over how to respond. The truth was, I'd felt a growing excitement over the party. Not only because I couldn't wait to see Nyssa's face when she opened the photo album I'd made for her, but also because tomorrow, Sawyer would finally be able to confess to being my Secret Santa.

"I have to admit," I said now. "The Secret Santa stuff was more fun than I thought it would be."

He looked at me curiously. "Don't tell me you're succumbing to the Hallmark brainwashing!"

"I'm not!" I blurted, but even as I said it, my chest tightened. I found myself doing this more and more with Sawyer lately, scrambling to prove that I was who I said I was. I took a deep breath. "It's just that, I can't wait to meet my Secret Santa face-to-face. Finally."

"I hope you won't be disappointed," Sawyer said as the bell rang. He stood up to throw his trash away and held out his hand to help me up off the floor.

"I don't think I will be," I said breathlessly, my hand tingling in his.

"There's only one part of the party I'm looking forward to." He smiled. "Hanging out with you." He gave my hand a slight squeeze, then turned to join Gabe to walk to class. "See you later."

I was still staring after him, knees wobbling, heart prancing, when Jez latched onto me.

"I saw hand-holding!" she whisper-shrieked. "Hand-holding. In the middle of the caf!"

"I know!" I said. "But it's—" I paused, focusing on the tiles passing under my feet. "It's different from what I expected. I kind of get the feeling he'd like me less if I didn't agree with him on everything."

"But you guys *do* agree on everything."

Did we? Really? My stomach churned with uncertainty.

"You know what?" Jez slid an arm around me. "You're

nervous. That's all. Who wouldn't be? You're about to become the girlfriend of one of the coolest guys in school. And you've never had a real boyfriend before! This is huge."

I looked at her enthusiastic smile and felt a wave of relief. "You're right." I smiled back at her. "I'm sure that's all it is."

On Thursday, school went by in a buzz of excitement, as everyone prepared for the last day before the weeklong winter recess. No official announcement had been made about school being canceled for Friday, but weather stations were predicting the snowstorm was going to dump at least six inches or more, so teachers were handing out candy canes and showing movies on their Smart Boards in full last-day-before-break mode.

The expectant, cheery atmosphere made it even harder for me to focus on anything besides the party, and each hour passed with excruciating slowness as my restlessness grew. By the time the final bell rang and kids streamed out of the school, whooping and hollering at the heavy blanket of clouds overhead, my pulse was racing.

When I got to the Leaning Tower of Pizza, where the party was being held, I found everyone from the homeroom class hanging out in a private room in the back. I had to hand it to Mrs. Finnegan. She'd gone all out for this party. Strings of lights and twinkling snowflakes hung down from the ceiling, casting the room in a soft, multicolored glow. The old-fashioned jukebox in the back corner was playing Sinatra's version of "Silver Bells," and there was even a floor-to-ceiling tree decked out with decorations.

Underneath the tree were everyone's final Secret Santa presents, which we'd brought into school earlier in the week in shopping bags so no one would sneak peeks. They shone in sparkling piles, and even though the logical part of me tried to quell it, I felt the same stirrings of unstoppable eagerness I felt when I was little on Christmas morning. Maybe presents were materialistic, but when it came down to it, they were pretty darn irresistible, too.

"Isn't it exciting?" Nyssa said, coming to stand beside me. She was as glam as ever in a bright red sweaterdress that looked like it was at least part cashmere. "My parents don't even bother to wrap presents anymore. They don't see the point. I usually just get a cash card in my stocking."

"Really?" I said. "That's . . . different." *And sad*, I thought automatically, then caught myself. Wait a sec. Wasn't I always telling my parents I didn't see the point of lots of gifts under the tree when so many other people in the world went without? Still, imagining Nyssa opening a slender envelope of money made a pang shoot through my heart.

Nyssa flipped her hair over her shoulder. "I feel ridiculous complaining about it, really. I should be grateful. But it takes away the fun of the surprise, you know?"

"I get that," I said. "But, hey, speaking of surprises, how did the one for Sawyer work out?"

"Great!" She grinned. "Thanks again for the idea. My dad is setting up the tour for a day when Brittle Bones will be recording an album."

"Brittle Bones is his favorite band! He'll love it," I said.

"Maybe he'll invite you on the tour with him," Nyssa said slyly with a giggle.

"Yeah." My heart sped up, but instead of the dizzying joy I'd expected, I felt a mild sense of panic.

But I didn't have time to dwell on it, because at that second, Nyssa sucked in a breath and whispered, "Oh!" She put a finger to her lips. "He just walked in!"

Sawyer spotted me from across the room, smiled, and took a step toward me, but Mrs. Finnegan walked in right behind him.

"All right, ladies and gentlemen, have a seat where you are, please." She bounced on the tips of her toes. "I'll pass out the presents, and we'll open them together. Once you've opened your gift, you can move about the room to thank your Secret Santas."

Excited whispers swirled around the room as Mrs. Finnegan handed out the presents. Adrenaline surged through me when she settled a heavy square package, covered in gold wrapping paper with dark angels printed all over it, into my lap. My body tensed with excitement. I could barely breathe. I knew Sawyer was sitting somewhere off to my left, but I didn't have the courage to look at him.

"That's everyone," Mrs. Finnegan announced, beaming. "On the count of three. One, two . . ."

"Three" was drowned out by the commotion of twenty-two presents being ripped open. I eagerly tore off the gold wrapping paper and lifted the lid of the plain brown box. Inside, nestled in purple tissue paper, was the digital camera I'd been trying to save for, along with a note that read: *"It is more important to click with people than to click the shutter." Happy Holidays, Sawyer.*

I knew that quote. Alfred Eisenstaedt, one of my favorite photographers, had said that. I'd never thought of it as romantic, until I saw it scrawled in Sawyer's handwriting. Did he mean click with people, as in click with *him*? I smiled. I couldn't have dreamed up anything more perfect he could've said to me.

I lifted the camera out of the box as gently as I would've done with a precious crystal, turning it over in my hands, examining its features as my smile grew even wider. I was about to turn the camera on when I was suddenly attacked by a squealing, hugging red sweater that wouldn't let me go.

"Omigod, Em!" Nyssa cried, her lip-glossed smile looking

172

even more fabulous in its beaming authenticity. "*You're* my Secret Santa?"

"Guilty," I deadpanned, but I couldn't help laughing as she threw her arms around me again.

"This," she said, lovingly patting the photo album cradled in one arm, "is the best present I've ever gotten. *Ever.*"

"Oh, come on," I joked, "it's no competition for Coach or cashmere."

"Would you stop and let me give you a compliment, please?" Nyssa said, turning serious. "This album, the cookies you made, the funny shirt. All the gifts you gave me were so, so thoughtful. Seriously. I've heard you say how much you hate the holidays, but honestly, Em, you're the best gift giver ever." She squeezed my hand, looking shockingly teary-eyed with joy. "Thank you."

"You're welcome." Warmth filled me, and I felt relief and pride that I'd made her so sincerely happy with such simple gifts.

"I'm going to go get a slice of pizza," she said, then leaned forward to add in a whisper, "because you're about to get some company." She hurried across the room as Sawyer walked over to me, smiling.

"The so-called secret's out," he said, nodding toward the camera. "Do you like it?"

"I love it," I said softly. "Thank you. All of your Secret Santa ideas were awesome."

"I'm glad, but I can't take the credit. I got some great tips from one of your friends."

"Really?" I said, instantly thinking how sneaky Jez was to be able to pull the wool over my eyes for this long. And she'd denied it, the stinker. "So that's how you knew that I wanted a new camera?"

He nodded, then motioned toward the note he'd written, which I was holding in my hand. "That's also how I found out about Eisenstaedt. I didn't have a clue who he was, or about that quote, either. Your friend did all the shopping and card writing for me. With all the prep work I had to do for the concert, I didn't have any time."

"Oh." A heavy disappointment filled me, but I immediately tried to shake it off. So what if he hadn't chosen the gifts on his own? That didn't make them any less sweet. "Well, I'm glad my friend could help," I said, determined not to feel let down by what were probably my impossibly high expectations. "I so needed a new camera."

"That's what I was told." He nodded. "It's not exactly brand-new, though. I had to get it discounted. It came used from some online store."

"It's great," I said, meaning it. "And what about *your* final Secret Santa gift? Are you happy with it?"

"Some labels are so corrupt, but still, I've never been to a studio before. It'll be cool." He smiled, leaning toward me. "I know you helped with it. Nyssa told me."

I blushed. "I tried to come up with things you'd like . . ."

"You did. You know me pretty well. Probably better than I know you." He leaned toward me and whispered, "Maybe we can work on that?"

Yes, please, I wanted to say, but my voice was lost somewhere between my spinning head and pounding pulse. Before I could find it, the overhead lights brightened and the music died away as Mrs. Finnegan stepped into the center of the room.

"I'm so sorry to interrupt the festivities," she said, "but I'm afraid we're going to have to cut the party short on account of weather." She gestured toward the window, where snow flurries were swirling across the purpling sky. "The storm's starting earlier than expected, and the school's notified your parents to pick you up."

Groans and protests rose up around the room as Mrs. Finnegan ushered everyone out into the hallway to get their coats. I hung back beside Sawyer, frustrated at having to leave the party right when Sawyer and I seemed to be on the threshold of something big.

We walked outside into the steadily cascading snow and watched as most of the rest of the class got into waiting cars. As Nyssa's au pair pulled to the curb, Nyssa surprised me by hugging me again.

"Merry Christmas, Em," she said, then pulled back, slapping a hand over her mouth. "Oh, I forgot you hate it. Um, 'Merry Grinchmas'?"

"Nice try." I laughed. "I'll take the 'Merry Christmas.' Just this once." I waved as she slid into the car.

It was only after her car had disappeared that I realized Sawyer and I were alone on the sidewalk. My pulse roared as I turned to see him watching me, smiling.

Sawyer glanced skyward, blinking into the snowflakes. "I never thought I'd say this, but I'm sorry the party's over."

"Sad to leave behind all the Chipmunks' Christmas carols?" I teased.

My heart bounded into my throat when he shook his head, his tawny eyes darkening with sincerity. "No," he said softly, "sad to leave you."

"Oh," I whispered, weak-kneed.

He took a step closer. "I'd like to see you sometime over winter break."

"That would be great," I said breathlessly.

He smiled. "This Saturday? We could go to the movies."

"Ooh, yes!" I cried. "There's a showing of Bela Lugosi's *Dracula* at Vintage Cinemas. I love that version."

"Vampires? Not my fave." His forehead crinkled in distaste. "I was actually thinking about the documentary on Blink-182?"

"Sure!" I said enthusiastically. It didn't sound like as much fun, but I could always catch Lugosi another time. What I wanted took a backseat to the idea of my first official date with Sawyer. I grinned, then shivered involuntarily as a gust of bitter wind blew down the street, whisking my black trilby hat right off my head. I rushed down the sidewalk after it, but Sawyer beat me to it. I started to reach for it, but he gently slid it back onto my head.

"That was a heroic rescue," I said.

"Nah." He shook his head. "You don't need rescuing." He smiled, and then, in a gesture that took my breath away, turned up the corners of my coat collar, and still holding onto them, gently eased me toward him. "But it gave me an excuse to get closer, so I could do this."

"Do what?" I could feel myself trembling as I asked the question.

He leaned toward me, and my eyes closed instinctively as my heart pummeled my chest. I'd dreamed of this, and now the moment was here. But at the last second, when we were so close I felt the warmth of his breath, I panicked and turned my face to the side. His lips brushed against my cheek.

Heated embarrassment coursed through me, and we both pulled back in surprise.

"Sorry," I blustered, peering worriedly into his bewildered eyes. "I didn't mean to—"

"No worries," he said nonchalantly. "Practice makes perfect, right?" His voice was its easygoing self, but there was a tautness underneath its surface. He tucked his hands into his coat pockets and took a step back.

"Um . . . yeah." My heart sank. Of all the times I'd imagined what it would be like to kiss Sawyer, none of them had included a slipup of this magnitude. I tried to close up the space between us, determined to give it another go, even if it meant that I made the first move. But he peered over my shoulder as sweeping headlights brightened his face.

"I think that's your mom?" He nodded toward the street, and I sighed as Mom pulled up, waving at me to climb in.

"So . . . Saturday?" I asked hesitantly, hoping I hadn't botched the kiss so badly that he was having second thoughts about our date.

"Definitely," he said, giving me a reassuring smile. "I'll text you with showtimes tomorrow."

"Okay." Relief washed over me, but after the car pulled away into the slushy street, I sank back against the seat, cringing. My first kiss ever. My first kiss with the most perfect boy in the world, and it hadn't even been a kiss as much as an awkward peck on the cheek. How could something so delicious in my dreams be such a disaster in real life?

Chapter Eleven

"What do you mean, the kiss was bad?" Jez's screech was so incredulous, I had to hold the phone away from my ear.

"It wasn't even really a kiss." I flopped back against the pillows of my bed, tucking my blanket tighter around me to ward off the chill that seemed to be permeating every corner of our house. Outside, the snow was falling thick and fast. "He got my cheek."

"Because you *moved*! Do we need to review the rules for kissing? When a guy is coming in for a landing, you don't move the runway!"

"I know." I groaned. "I sort of froze." I shifted uncomfortably on the bed, remembering the weird hesitation that had come over me just before his lips met mine. I tried to pull up any recollection of fireworks or blazing sparks I could find. There wasn't a trace . . . not even a fizzle.

"Em." Jez was all seriousness now. "This is just your expectations meshing with reality. You've spent so much time dreaming about this, there's no way it could possibly live up to the fairy tale you created in your head. And now that you've gotten the first kiss over with, the second one can only be better."

"Absolutely," I said, feeling an inkling of confidence returning. "By the way, thanks for helping Sawyer with my gifts. The camera is amazing!"

"What?"

"He told me one of my friends gave him Secret Santa pointers." I smiled into the phone. "You denied it before, but now the secret's out. It had to be you."

There was surprised silence on the other end of the line. "It wasn't, Em. I swear. He didn't talk to me about the Secret Santa stuff at all."

My brow furrowed. "But if you didn't help him, who did?"

"Don't know. Maybe Lyra? Or Nyssa?"

"Maybe," I mumbled. But did Lyra or Nyssa know me well enough to give Sawyer such dead-on suggestions? I wasn't sure.

I was interrupted by a knock sounding on my bedroom door. I lifted my head off the pillow to see Mom sticking her head around the door, motioning for me to come downstairs.

"Jez, I gotta go," I said into the phone. "I'll call you tomorrow?"

"Sure," she said. "It's looking like it'll definitely be a snow day!"

Once I hung up the phone, the pitching of my insides returned. Each time I thought about the missed kiss, heated embarrassment filled me. Trying to shake it off, I went downstairs to see what Mom needed. I found her in her office, frantically printing out pictures and burning files onto CDs. Piles of order forms and papers were scattered across the floor.

"Whoa." I took in the mess. "Did the storm blow through here, too?"

"Funny," Mom mumbled, her eyes never shifting from her computer screen. "No. I'm trying to get these orders printed and ready before the weather gets any worse. I'm supposed to drop off a bunch of holiday cards at people's houses tomorrow. But with the storm, who knows if the power will hold out."

"Really?" I glanced at the window to see snow piling up rapidly on its sill. "I didn't think it was supposed to be that bad."

"I don't know." Her voice had a frazzled edge. "It's coming down hard already."

The wind gave a low moan, and I instinctively flipped up the hood of my sweatshirt. "Um, did you need my help with something?"

Mom snapped her fingers, as if she'd just remembered. "Yes! Hot cider. Could you make your dad a cup? He's down in the basement. I've tried everything to get him out of this funk he's in, but right now I've got so much to do. Maybe you could cheer him up—"

"Sure," I said quickly, knowing that I was mostly responsible for his funk to begin with. "Do you want some, too?" It was what we always did on snowy nights like this. Dad usually lit a fire and we sat around the Christmas tree, sipping cider and playing cheesy board games. "I'm going to make myself a cup."

"Not right now." She flipped through her papers, muttering to herself.

I left Mom to her chaos, made two cups of cider, and headed for the basement. The second I reached the bottom stair, I regretted it. Dad was in his recliner, his eyes on the television, his smile even sadder than usual. When I glanced at the screen, I understood why. There was six-year-old me, clad in pajamas and laughing wildly on Christmas morning as I raced to the pile of presents under the tree. As I tore open the first package, Grandma scooped me onto her lap, kissing the top of my head while I unwrapped a doll.

"I forgot all about that doll," I said, suddenly remembering that I'd called her Posy. "I took her everywhere with me."

Dad gave a start at seeing me there in the room, and then he nodded. "Grandma went to a dozen toy stores to find that doll. It was sold out almost everywhere. But she wouldn't rest until she got one for you."

"I didn't know that," I said quietly.

Dad sighed. "Look at that smile." He stared at the wide-eyed, giggling little girl filling the screen. "Magic."

I felt a pang of guilt, and looked away from the television. "I brought you some cider," I offered, holding it out to him.

He shook his head. "Thanks, but my heartburn's acting up tonight, so I'll pass."

"Oh. Okay." I searched for something cheery to say. "Well, do you want to come upstairs? If you're lucky, I might even let you beat me in a round of Christmas-opoly."

Dad glanced up in surprise. "You hate that game."

I shrugged. "As long as you don't start doing Jimmy Stewart impressions halfway through, I'll survive."

He laughed softly, and for a second, he looked like he was going to get up. Then he shook his head. "No, it's all right. Go on back upstairs. Don't worry about me."

My heart sagged. "Okay," I said. "Let me know if you change your mind." I took the stairs slowly, my spirits fading. This was what I'd wanted for months—a Christmas without Hallmark fanfare and campy traditions. But without my dad's schoolboy excitement, without the eye rolls I exchanged with Mom over his ridiculous parodies of Christmas carols and his recitations from *It's a Wonderful Life*, everything felt wrong. As I passed the family room on the way to the kitchen, my eyes fell on the darkened fireplace, and I shivered. This time, more from loneliness than cold.

His head bent toward me, and his arms wrapped around my shoulders. His face was in shadow, but I knew it was right. His lips came close to mine. My heart bubbled with happiness and expectation, and . . .

"Em!" The voice broke through my delicious reverie. "Emery, sweetie. Wake up!"

I reluctantly opened my eyes, feeling instant disappointment. It was morning, I was in my bed, and Mom was standing at the door, calling my name.

It had only been a dream.

"Hey, sleepyhead," Mom said. "Good news, school is canceled! But Dad and I are going out for a bit."

"Huh?" I tried to shake off my drowsiness. "Why?"

"It's still snowing. Coming down steady." Mom motioned to the window, and I could see at least a foot piled up on the rooftops across the street. "But I've got to deliver these orders. We're going now, just in case the roads turn icy." She turned to the hallway. "We'll be back by lunch."

"Okay, bye," I mumbled, flopping back onto the pillow. I was glad to have a snow day; it made me feel like a little kid.

A few minutes later, I heard the rumble of Dad's SUV pulling out of the driveway. Yanking the covers over my head, I tried to go back to sleep. But after tossing and turning for a while, I finally gave up, got dressed, and trudged downstairs for some cereal.

As I ate, the loneliness I'd felt last night returned. Without Mom and Dad, the house was too quiet. I picked up my cell to call Jez, then stopped. I realized, with a jolt of surprise, that it wasn't Jez I really wanted to talk to right now. I think I knew why. There was someone else I was really missing.

I dumped the rest of my cereal, scribbled a note to my parents, grabbed my sled from the garage, and headed down the sidewalk, hoping he'd be home.

My heart sped up as I climbed the steps to his front porch, and I hesitated before knocking, suddenly feeling all my nerve rush out of me.

I held my breath as I heard the lock turning from the inside, and when Alex opened the door, my heart leapt. It was so good to see him, and I was struck with how cute he looked. It stunned me for a moment, but a second later, I broke into a wide smile. He didn't return it, but I swallowed and pressed on.

I held out the thermos I'd brought with me. "Before you say anything, it's *not* hot chocolate. Mine would never stand up to the competition."

"You're right about that," he said gruffly. He was doing his best to look grumpy, but he was having a hard time pulling it off. I hadn't realized until this moment how much I'd missed him.

"It's hot apple cider," I said, nodding toward the thermos. "A peace offering. And," I added as the wind blew a fresh wave of snow right into my face, "possibly a bribe for you to let me come in? I'm standing in a polar vortex here."

He performed a perfect eye roll, and if I hadn't been so afraid he might shut the door in my face, I would've told him I was proud. "Come in," he finally said, swinging the door open wider.

"Thanks," I said in relief. Once I was standing in his kitchen, with him waiting, arms crossed, I knew I had to keep going. I took a deep breath and spoke again. "I came over to say I'm sorry. I lost my temper last week. I said things I didn't mean. I don't always agree with what you think. But"—I heaved a sigh—"can we make up? Because the thing is"—I looked into his softening eyes, my heart racing—"I miss you."

He was quiet for a long minute, focusing on emptying the thermos into two cups, and my stomach tensed with worry. I didn't know what I'd do if he didn't accept my apology. Finally, his face relaxed a bit, and he handed me my cup.

"You make it tough to say no, Em," he finally said with a sigh. "I'm sorry, too. I need to learn to keep my mouth shut. Maybe I give too much advice."

"You do," I said, elbowing him. "But some of it's pretty dead-on. Listening to you is sort of like eating vegetables. I don't always want to do it, but deep inside, I know it's good for me."

He stared at me over his cup, and then we both burst out laughing.

"That might have been the most offensive compliment I've ever heard," he said when he finally caught his breath.

"You know what I mean, don't you?"

"Yeah." He grinned, and this time there was nothing hesitant about it. "And"—his eyes turned serious—"I missed you, too."

My face warmed under his gaze, and I scrambled for a way to lighten things up. "Yeah, well, I *didn't* miss you giving me the hot chocolate hard sell all the time."

He took a sip of his cider. "This is good. But hot chocolate's better."

I snorted. "You'll never learn when to quit, will you?"

His eyes glinted with challenge. "Neither will you."

"And here I thought I'd find you weak and vulnerable from being sick."

He shook his head. "Oh no. Abuelo had me take a temazcal herb steam treatment, and I'm way better." In response to what must have been my blank look, he added, "It's an old Oaxacan tradition."

"Oh, cool. So, if you're feeling better, do you think you'd be up for some sledding? I walked by the hill at Main Street Park, and it's got at least two feet of hard-packed snow now." That spot was my dad's favorite sledding hill.

Alex nodded enthusiastically. "I've been cooped up in this house all week. Sounds great. Just let me go upstairs and get the okay from Abuelo."

"Tell him I promise not to throw any snowballs at your poor stuffy nose unless you really deserve it."

"My nose isn't stuffy anymore." Alex laughed as he headed for the stairs in the foyer. "And I don't think it's *me* he's going to be worried about."

"Truce!" I cried as another snowball smacked me on the head. I sputtered, wiping snow off my frozen lips. "Hey, have you no mercy? I'm calling a truce!"

Another snowball flew toward me, and I ducked behind the sled, using it as a barricade.

"Didn't you know I'm going to be a pitcher for the school base-ball team?" Alex called to me as another snowball whizzed by, nearly missing my shoulder.

"No!" I called back through my laughter. "I'm not exactly up on the sports extracurriculars, remember?"

"Well, that was before you met me. I expect you to come to at least one game."

Lying under the sled for protection, I shimmied on my stom-ach toward the tree. "I can probably live with a baseball game or two, as long as I'm not forced into any spirit wear."

"Hey, if you ever wore anything with the school mascot on it, I'd be disappointed."

I lifted up the edge of the sled for long enough to launch a snowball his way, hitting him square in the back. "Gotcha!" I shouted gleefully, then jumped up with the sled to run for the steep hill on the outskirts of Main Street Park. If I could beat him to the top, maybe I could sled down again before he fired his armful of snowballs at me. Breathless and laughing, I made it to the crest of the hill, jumped on the sled, and pushed off with my hands. The sled picked up speed as it whooshed downward, and I raised my fist in a victory pump as I got closer to Alex, who was still running uphill.

"Not so fast, show-off!" He grinned wickedly, dropped every snowball but one, and made a dive for the sled. I shrieked as he sat down behind me and grabbed me around the waist, then crushed a snowball right on top of my hat.

"Hey!" I yelled, squirming away. The right side of the sled tilted, throwing me off-balance.

"Watch out!" Alex hollered. "We're going to tip—"

Suddenly, I was airborne, the wind whistling in my ears as the ground rushed toward me. I hit the snow and tumbled straight into Alex, who was sprawled a few feet away. I closed my eyes on impact, and then lay there laughing so hard that the only sound I could make was a panting wheeze.

I opened my eyes to see Alex's face inches from mine, his breath warm on my cheek, his eyes full of laughter. It felt like we were connected by some force pulling us together, but in a good way. Not like the nervous uncertainty I felt around Sawyer. There was a fresh, soapy scent to Alex's skin, and starbursts of gold around his pupils, like drops of honey in pools of chocolate. How had I never noticed how cool his eyes were before?

"Are you still alive?" Alex murmured.

I shook off my confusion of emotions and focused on reality by giving him a playful smack on the back of his head. "I might be, if you would get *off* me." I shoved him gently away so that I could sit up, then glared at him. "You fight dirty."

He grinned, shrugging. "Who ever said snowball fights had to be fair?"

I was already packing a snowball behind my back, ready to launch a surprise attack, but the wind suddenly screamed across the hill with such force that I had to put out a hand to brace myself. Alex scooted closer to me to act as a windbreak, and for a minute, both of us tucked our faces into our jacket collars to ward off the stinging snow.

"Where did that come from?" I said when the howling died down enough for my voice to be heard.

Alex glanced up at the sky. "I don't remember the clouds being so dark when we first got here. Do you?"

I shook my head. Sure enough, the sky was a heavy gray, and

the snow was whipping around us furiously, starting to blow into drifts at the base of the hill. "The storm was supposed to be ending by now."

"Looks like it's getting worse." Alex stood up and offered me a hand. "We should go. I'll walk you home."

The clouds grew more ominous as we walked, and in the few minutes it took us to reach the other side of the park, the snow was falling so heavily I could only see a foot or two in front of me. As we ducked our heads into the bitter wind and pushed on, I was glad we were only a few blocks from my house. But gladder to have Alex beside me. It was getting harder to see, and when Alex reached out his hand to me, I took it, the steady pressure of his fingers in mine grounding me in the blinding snow.

Finally, I saw glowing colors through the blanket of white, and relief rushed through me.

"The Holly Jolly House!" I yelled over the wind. I'd never thought it could happen, but I was actually happy for the thousands of lights guiding us home. As we got to our front yard, I saw Dad struggling to right some reindeer that had fallen over in the wind and were already half-buried in snow.

He waved us toward the house, yelling, "Everything's blowing over! I'm trying to stake a few things down."

Alex offered to help, but Dad shook his head.

"It's getting too cold. You two go inside. I won't stay out much longer."

We nodded, and climbed the front porch steps, bracing ourselves against the fierce wind. Mom met us at the door.

"Thank goodness," she said, hugging us both in relief. "I was about to send Dad out to get you." She gestured to the TV, which was on the weather channel. "It's a full-blown blizzard. Caught everyone by surprise." She turned to Alex. "I called your grandfather, and he's walking over. I tried to convince him to stay home, but he said it would be a good excuse to try out his new snowshoes."

Alex rolled his eyes. "That sounds like Abuelo."

I slid the scarf down from my mouth and grinned at Alex, who was covered head to toe in white. "You could pass for an abominable snowman."

"Look who's talking, ice queen."

"Both of you need to get changed and warmed up before you

197

catch a cold," Mom said as a blast of wind shook the shutters on the front of the house. "Alex, I'll bring you some of Mr. Mason's clothes. They'll be big, but at least they're dry."

The door blew open, and Dad hobbled in, caked in snow and clutching his back.

"Oh no, honey," Mom said, rushing to offer him a shoulder to lean on. "Your back?"

"Some of the lights blew down and I was trying to fix them," he said through clenched teeth. "I must've twisted the wrong way . . ." He took another step and winced.

Mom rolled her eyes at Alex and me as if to say, *I told him so.* "Come on," she told Dad, holding him up. "Straight upstairs for you."

Dad made a sorry attempt at shaking his head. "I've got to get them up before the Holiday Stroll—"

"The Holiday Stroll will have to survive with one less strand of lights," Mom interrupted. She started for the stairs with her arm around Dad just as the lights inside flickered once, then went out.

"Power's out!" I cried. Everything was coated in stormy gray shadows—the lights both inside the house and out.

"Wow," Alex said. "We never got these in California."

"There's a fire going in the family room," Mom said as she and Dad took one painstaking step at a time. "If you're careful, you can roast marshmallows in the fireplace. Em, light the candles on the mantel. I'll check on you two in a bit. May as well get comfy. We're in for quite a storm."

Chapter Twelve

I bit into the gooey center of my s'more and smiled in satisfaction. "Mmmm. Perfect."

The wind was still howling, and snow pelted the windows of the family room. It was hard to see how much more snow had fallen since darkness was coming, but when Mom opened the door to let Señor Perez inside, there was at least another foot covering the porch steps. Mom had already decided Alex and his grandpa were staying the night, since the whiteout conditions made it too dangerous for them to walk home. Now there was muffled chatter from the kitchen, where Mom and Alex's grandfather were busy cooking chicken with mole sauce for dinner.

"A traditional Oaxacan meal," Señor Perez had said as Mom had manually lit our gas stove.

I'd never heard of mole sauce before, but the smells from the kitchen were enticing, and along with the glow from the candles and fireplace, they filled the house with a coziness that even the blackout couldn't quench. Alex and I had been sitting in front of the fire, wrapped in blankets and talking for over an hour. After not seeing each other for a whole week, we both had a lot to say. It was so great filling him in on school, and telling him the latest kiddie sagas about the North Pole Wonderland.

There was one topic I made a point of avoiding, though. Sawyer. Sawyer was part of the reason Alex and I had gotten into that fight in the first place, and we were having such a good time tonight, I didn't want to ruin it.

Now I glanced at Alex, who was blowing out his flaming marshmallow, and laughed.

"You can make hot chocolate, but you sure can't make s'mores," I told him.

I took the wire hanger we used as a skewer from his hand, tossed the charred remains of the marshmallow onto a paper plate, and took a fresh one out of the bag.

"Watch and learn," I teased as I held the marshmallow above the flames.

"I thought you didn't like my hot chocolate," he said as I handed him a s'more with my perfectly toasted marshmallow inside.

"I don't," I said. "But the masses sure seem to."

"And since when do you care what the masses think?"

I grinned. "Hey, I didn't say they were *right*."

He clutched his chest and fell back against the couch pillows. "Like a dagger to the heart." I rolled my eyes, and he threw a pillow at me, which I ducked just in time. He smiled. "I haven't given up on you. I'll make you fall in love with my hot chocolate yet."

I didn't know why, but hearing Alex say the words "fall in love" made my face feel warm. I tried to push that feeling away. "I wish you would quit trying to change me," I told him instead.

Suddenly, his face turned serious in the firelight. "I don't want you to change. I want you to stop trying so hard not to. Sometimes I think you put up a fight just for the sake of proving a point."

I opened my mouth to argue, then stopped myself. It would be proving him right if I did. "Okay, bring it on," I challenged. "What do you want me to do, right now? Something you think I'd normally hate. Name it, and I'll do it."

Alex rubbed his hands together, plotting, then snapped his fingers. "I've got it." He grabbed my tablet off the coffee table. "Watch *It's a Wonderful Life* with me. Right here. Right now. Tonight. No excuses."

I buried my head in the couch cushion and groaned. "I knew it was going to involve Christmas."

I lifted my head, making sure Alex got a good look at my exaggerated frown as he scooted beside me and set the tablet on his knees.

"Hey, you got yourself into this, remember?" He pressed the tablet to wake it up. "You will survive. I promise. You might *even* enjoy it."

I wanted to grit my teeth, to tell him there wasn't a chance he'd be right. But once the movie began, and the first half hour had passed, I forgot every argument I had against the movie. Dialogue I'd been so quick to roll my eyes at in the past, for some reason tonight, struck me as sweet. It might've been because, as I watched, I imagined Grandma sitting beside me on the couch telling me she'd give me the moon if I wanted it, just like George had told Mary in the movie. I could see my dad beside her, grinning like he was thirty years younger than he actually was, without a worry in the world. How many times had we all watched this movie together when I was little? At least a dozen.

Or, it might've been because of Alex. Watching the movie with him was like watching it for the first time, seeing everything with his fresh enthusiasm. Everything about his laugh and smile as he watched was genuine, and weird as it was, knowing that he loved the movie as much as he did made me want to like it just so that I could share it with him.

Soon, I was making comments about mean Mr. Potter right alongside Alex, giggling at Clarence's angelic innocence, and rooting for George to return to his old life again. There was one fleeting moment when I felt a pang of nerves, imagining what Sawyer would say about me watching this movie, but I quickly brushed it off. Sawyer might not understand, but then again, we didn't have to agree on everything, did we?

I snuggled into the blanket, feeling the kind of satisfying physical tiredness that comes after spending time outdoors in the snow. A peaceful sleepiness swept over me, and before I knew it, I was struggling to keep my eyes open. Just as I was drifting off, a thought struck me. It didn't matter how much Alex and I disagreed on, or how different we were. I didn't ever want to risk losing him again.

"Dinner!"

Mom's voice was distant, muted, and I was wrapped in such a pleasant cocoon of warmth that I didn't want to move. I yawned and shifted slightly, and when I did, my heart jumped to my throat. My head wasn't on a pillow. It was . . . on Alex's shoulder. His head was nestled into mine, his eyes closed in sleep.

Blushing like mad, I eased away, but when I did, Alex's head slumped back against the couch, and his eyes opened. I hoped I'd moved away before he could realize that we'd fallen asleep head to head like a—what? *Couple*, my brain said in turmoil.

"Hey," he said, smiling. "Some life of the party I am, huh? Sorry. I didn't mean to fall asleep."

"No, it's fine," I blurted. Good. He didn't know.

He nodded, yawning. "So, I meant to ask you before, but then we got caught up in sledding and everything. What was your last Secret Santa gift? Did you like it?"

I swallowed thickly, feeling a stirring of dread. This was it, the perfect time to tell him everything that had happened with Sawyer. The topic I'd been avoiding all day.

I took a deep breath. "The gift was amazing," I started. "A new camera. Well, not new, but new enough . . ."

"And you're happy with it?" he asked, his eyes intent on my face.

"Are you kidding?" I laughed in my nervousness. "It's incredible! I mean, I haven't had a chance to work with it yet, but it's the camera I wanted. Definitely."

"That's great."

I nodded, ducking my head to stare into the roaring fire. My hands clenched and unclenched in my lap, but I gave my best attempt at an excited smile. "There's something else, too," I tried to gush. "Sawyer asked me to the movies! Tomorrow night. Or, we're supposed to go out tomorrow night if the storm's over—" My words died away awkwardly, and I felt a surge of irritation with myself. Why had the happiness in my voice sounded so fake?

"That's big news," Alex said slowly, but his voice was weighted down with disappointment. "I know how much you want this."

"Oh, I do!" I said as confidently as I could, even though that was far from what I felt.

Alex looked thoughtful, then frowned. "Well, we won't see much of each other anymore, I guess."

I snorted in disbelief. "Of course we will."

He raised an eyebrow. "No. Once Christmas is over and the North Pole Wonderland closes, you won't be working at the mall anymore. And we never hang out at school." He shrugged. "Things will change."

"I won't let them," I said, fighting down an inkling of unease. This week had felt so disjointed without Alex, and now I wasn't able to fathom a day when we wouldn't talk or see each other. I opened my mouth to tell him he was wrong, but at that moment, Mom stuck her head into the family room.

"Oh, good, you're up!" she declared. "You guys looked adorable snoozing on the couch! I hated to wake you, but, Alex, your grandfather has made the most magnificent meal."

"You were sleeping, too?" Alex shot me a questioning glance.

"Um, not really," I mumbled, my cheeks on fire. I leapt up to follow Mom into the kitchen, desperately seeking a subject change. "How's Dad?"

Mom shook her head. "Terrible. I swear, he's more worried about those decorations than his back, stubborn man." She sighed. "If he could move, he'd be out in the yard right now on a rescue mission. With as much wind and snow as we're getting, I can't believe we'll still have the town's Holiday Stroll tomorrow. But if there is a stroll, I'm afraid there won't be any Holly Jolly House left to see."

"Oh no," I said, and Mom glanced at me in surprise.

"I thought you'd be saying good riddance." Her words were

meant teasingly, but it hurt when she said them. "Are you having a change of heart?"

"I—I . . ." I wavered uncertainly. "I feel bad for Dad, that's all."

"Well, we'll see how things look in the morning." She squeezed my hand. "Now let's eat before it gets cold."

We sat down to the meal, which was delicious, just like Mom had said. But while Mom and Señor Perez seemed to have a never-ending stream of topics to chat about, Alex and I were completely tongue-tied. Short of a few clipped exchanges passing food and asking for seconds, neither one of us said much. Alex didn't offer any advice, like he usually did, or even crack any jokes about me being Grinchified. He ate quietly, and once we'd cleaned up the dinner dishes and Mom pulled out Scrabble, he stood to go to bed.

"Wait a sec!" I protested. "You're on my team. Your *abuelo* and my mom will cream me without you!"

He only shrugged. "I'm wiped after all that sledding." He waved with his flashlight as he headed upstairs to the guest bedroom he was sharing with Señor Perez. "See you in the morning."

My heart drooped as his footsteps sounded on the stairs, and even though Mom wanted to go ahead with the game, I excused myself a few minutes later, faking a yawn. "I'm going to head up, too."

Once I was tucked into bed under layers of blankets, all I could do was toss and turn. Usually my window was filled with the dancing, color-changing Christmas lights, but tonight the only view through the glass was darkness.

I squeezed my eyes shut, trying to summon excitement over my upcoming movie night with Sawyer. Still, all I could think about was my talk with Alex, and how strangely he'd behaved afterward. "Things will change," he'd said. Somehow, tonight, I felt like they'd already started to.

Chapter Thirteen

I woke up Saturday morning to a blinding brightness, and when I glanced at the window, I couldn't see the street because of the layer of ice and snow that had frozen to the glass overnight. I tried the light switch in my room. Nothing. The power was still out. After getting dressed, I hurried out of my room, my dread building with every step. Passing the open door to my parents' room, I peeked in. Dad was lying flat on his back on the bed, staring at the ceiling. His face told me everything I needed to know.

"Dad?" I whispered.

He sighed. "The Holly Jolly House is gone. Your mom took a look a few minutes ago. The storm blew most of it away."

My stomach dropped. I sat down beside him. "What are we going to do?" I figured he'd have a plan.

I felt even worse when I heard his barely perceptible "Nothing." The lines on his forehead deepened. "All the families who line up out there every year," he mumbled. "The kids that look forward to this each Christmas. I hate disappointing them."

"I'm sure there are still some decorations up around town," I tried. "The storm wouldn't have destroyed all of them."

His eyes flicked to me, but I could see he was making an effort not to move his neck too much for fear of the pain. "It was never about the decorations," he said. "It was about the magic of believing." He sighed. "The sheer fun of giving the gift of that to other people, of sharing it with them. Like your grandma and I used to share it with you."

I bit my lip, feeling it threatening to tremble. I'd never seen Dad look so utterly defeated before. I felt responsible. Sure, I hadn't had anything to do with the Holly Jolly House getting blown away, but how many times in the last couple of years had I wished it would disappear? I'd gotten exactly what I'd wanted, so why did I feel so lousy?

"Em, could you please go ask your mom to make me another cup of coffee?" he asked, then sighed again. "It's not the same drinking it through a straw, but she won't let me try to sit up yet. I'm practically a hostage."

I laughed a little at that, then nodded. As I turned toward the door, I glanced back at him. "I'm really sorry, Dad," I whispered. I didn't know I had any inkling of sentimentality left for the Holly Jolly House, but here I was, with tears threatening my eyes. There *was* magic in believing. I'd felt it as a child. With Grandma, more than anyone else. Wanting to take away the Holly Jolly House from the town was like destroying a little bit of that magic. It was like taking away a part of Grandma, all over again. Who would wish for that?

I stopped dead on the stairs. A scrooge, that's who. A scrooge like . . . me.

On shaking legs, I took the stairs two at a time back up to my bedroom, then flung open my closet door. Flinging piles of dirty clothes this way and that, I dug through the mess at the bottom of my closet until my hand brushed against the velvet jewelry box. It was still at the bottom of one of my coat pockets, just as I had left it.

I set it in my lap and carefully opened the lid, then caught my breath. The locket was smaller than I remembered it being, but still just as lovely. With shaking fingers, I opened it and as soon as I did, a small slip of paper fluttered out. Picking it up, I read:

Emery, my sweet girl,

You're upset with me for leaving, I know, but you must never lose faith. Each Christmas, in the lights, the singing, and the magic, look for me. I'll be there, with you always. I love you.

Grandma

Tears trickled down my cheeks as I clutched the locket to my chest. The words settled over me, and suddenly I felt my heart softening. This was what I'd needed to hear. The promise from her, that she'd never left at all.

I wiped my eyes, slipped the necklace over my head, then ran downstairs. I flung open the front door and stepped onto the porch. Dad was right. The Holly Jolly House lay scattered across the mountainous drifts in the yard.

"What are you doing with the door wide open?" Mom stuck her head outside, surveying the damage again. "What a mess. It's such a shame." She shook her head. "It doesn't matter anyway. The power's still out in town. I'm sure the Holiday Stroll will be canceled."

"But what if it's not?" I asked.

"Your dad can't put this place back together in time, and I don't know anybody else who will." She shrugged, then shivered. "Now come inside before you freeze."

I followed her in, telling her about Dad's request for coffee. But I took one last look at the wreck outside as I shut the door, and suddenly I knew what I needed to do.

A strange giddiness filled me as I scrambled into the kitchen.

"Where's Alex?" I asked, staring at the remains of two mostly eaten breakfasts on the table.

"He and his grandfather left right before you came downstairs," Mom said. "I thought he'd said good-bye to you."

I was already heading for the door, grabbing my coat and boots from the entryway as I went. "Gotta go, Mom!" I hollered as I yanked the door open. "Be back soon!"

I didn't wait for a response before I slammed the door shut and leapt off the porch, immediately sinking deep into the snow. *They can't have gotten far,* I thought as I made my way through the drifts, which were so deep sometimes it felt more like wading than walking. When I reached the sidewalk, I turned in the direction of their house and, after rounding the corner onto their street, spotted them slowly moving through the drifts.

"Alex! Wait!" I cried. He turned around, surprised and confused, and I doubled my pace, then laughed as I almost fell face-first into the snow in my rush to reach them. I caught myself, but not before I was up to my armpits in freshly fallen powder.

"Need some help?" Alex asked.

I wanted to be irritated at the laughter I heard rippling his voice, but mainly I was grateful.

"Laugh it up, but I need help," I said. "Lots of it."

His smile widened. "Tell me something I don't already know."

He pulled me to my feet, and the feel of his hand on mine sent shivers through me.

"Thanks," I said, straightening. Then I grabbed him by the shoulders, and his eyebrows shot upward in surprise. "I need you."

"You. Need me?" Was it just me, or were his cheeks turning red. Was it from the cold?

"Yes! I need your help." I grabbed his hand and began dragging him in the direction of my house, waving to his grandfather as I went. "Alex is coming with me!" I called to Señor Perez over my shoulder. "He'll be home later!"

"Okay!" Señor Perez waved back. "Be careful!"

"Where are we going?" Alex asked, peering at me curiously. "Wait a second, you look different. Weirdly . . . cheerful. What's going on?"

I rolled my eyes. "Isn't it obvious? I'm going to fix the Holly Jolly House. And you're going to help me."

Alex stopped in the snow, his mouth falling open. "But you . . . you hate that house."

I hesitated but then giggled, surprising even myself with the light, airy sound. "Not anymore. I can't let our yard stand empty if the Holiday Stroll happens tonight. I have to fix everything. My grandma would've wanted me to, and . . . I want to make her proud again. I need to do this for her, for my dad." I looked into his chocolate eyes and smiled. "And for me."

"I don't believe it." Alex shook his head, baffled. "Are you— are you de-Scrooged?"

"I don't know," I admitted bashfully. "Maybe I am." I shrugged, and my smile widened. "I guess Ebenezer wasn't the only one haunted by pesky Christmas spirits." I elbowed him.

Alex grinned. "I bet his weren't nearly as good-looking."

"Now you just sound arrogant," I teased.

I was so glad to see him acting normal after the awkwardness I'd felt between us last night. Still, though, I wanted to make sure we were okay. "Um, about our talk yesterday . . ."

Alex waved the words away. "We have more important things to worry about." A conflicted look crossed his face, and for a minute, it seemed like he had more to say. In the end, though, he shook his head, seeming to decide against it.

"Um . . . we better get going," I said slowly, unsure of what to make of his silence. "It's already after ten. And we only have six hours until the stroll starts."

"*If* it starts," Alex warned.

"Hey! That's the talk of skeptics." I shot him a scolding glance. "Remember. There's magic in believing." I smiled. "And for once, I do."

Three hours later, I wondered when the magic would kick in. Tugging off my hat to wipe the perspiration off my forehead, I surveyed the headway we'd made. It wasn't much. Using our shovels, we'd dug out several buried reindeer and the candy cane trail that had once led to Santa's workshop. When our backs and arms had gotten too tired, we took breaks to scour the neighborhood, searching for the decorations that had blown away. I'd found three penguins, and Alex discovered one of the singing polar bears dangling in a tree. Still, the front yard looked bare compared to what it had been only a day ago.

"We're not even close to ready," I said as Alex struggled to untangle a ball of knotted Christmas lights.

"One step at a time." He glanced around, then gave me an encouraging smile. "We'll get there."

"There you go with the never-ending optimism again." I tossed a snowball halfheartedly in his direction. "We need more than optimism. We need a miracle."

Just then, there was a deep rumbling from down the street, and I turned my head to see one of Fairview's Power & Light trucks rolling toward us. When it reached our house, the driver rolled down his window, shaking his head sadly at our front yard.

"I hoped the storm might've gone easy on this part of town, but no such luck, huh?" he said. "What a shame. My kids love your house. We stop here every year during the Holiday Stroll. It's one of our favorite traditions."

"Really?" I said, surprised. I mean, I'd seen the people lining up to see our house each year, but a tradition? That was different. That meant that our house wasn't some oddity people came to stare at; it was part of the memories families in Fairview made each year. I felt a sudden rush of pride. "Well," I said firmly, "I'll see your family here tonight."

The driver's brow furrowed. "Hate to say it, but there's not a chance we'll get all the town's power up by then." He rubbed his chin, thinking. "But . . . if you can promise me your house will be ready, I'll see what I can do to get power back to your street in time."

I glanced at Alex and saw new determination dawning in his eyes, just as I was sure it was in mine. We grinned at each other, and then I turned back to the driver. "I promise. We'll be ready."

The driver smiled. "Good. Nobody should miss out on the Holly Jolly House." He waved, calling out, "See you later!" as he drove away.

As soon as the truck turned the corner of our street, I swiveled on my heel and headed for the front door. I'd turned off my cell phone last night because the battery was critically low. But maybe, just maybe, I'd have enough juice left on the phone to send out some texts.

"Hey, where are you going?" Alex asked. "We have serious work to do."

"I know!" I called out as I hurried through the door to find my phone. "That's why we need some serious reinforcements."

Within a half hour of my text, Jez and about a dozen other

friends of ours and Alex's were spread across our front yard setting up decorations. Each of them had brought decorations from their own houses to contribute. Lyra had rescued Hector the Mouse from under someone's car, and Rafael brought a large, ornate menorah that his parents let him borrow. Nyssa had rallied the glee club and they'd shown up in full force pushing a very large, very expensive-looking golden sleigh in front of them. It was piled high with red-and-gold-foil-wrapped fake presents.

"This is amazing!" I cried. "We can put that front and center and harness the light-up reindeer to it." I grinned at her. "Thanks, Nyssa."

Nyssa giggled. "I doubt my mom will even notice it's missing from our front porch." She then elbowed me, saying quietly, "I can't believe you're doing all this for your dad. You might actually make it off the naughty list this year, Em."

I snorted. "It's not just for Dad. It's for everyone in Fairview."

"Wow." She narrowed her eyes at me. "Sounds like something melted your icy heart. Or maybe, somebody?" She smiled knowingly. "You and Sawyer were the last to leave the party yesterday. Was it true love's kiss that did the trick?"

"Nyssa!" I hissed, blushing. Alex, who was standing a few feet away hitching the reindeer to the sleigh, glanced up at hearing the question, and I felt his eyes on us. "Shhh! Yes, we kissed. Sort of. But you don't need to announce it to everyone."

"Why not?" she asked. "That's great!"

"Because I'm—I'm not ready," I stammered, feeling more flustered than ever. Suddenly, I didn't want to talk about the kiss in front of Alex. Not now. Not ever.

Nyssa blew out a breath. "That makes no sense. You got the guy you wanted. Why keep it a secret? Unless . . ." She studied my face until I had to drop my eyes. "He *is* the guy you want, right?"

"Sure maybe," I blurted, shaking my head. "I mean, I don't know?"

Nyssa glanced up at the sky in exasperation. "If you don't know, then maybe you need to ask yourself what it is that's holding you back. And you better make up your mind soon, because there are hearts on the line here—"

"Hearts?" I repeated. "Plural? What do you mean—"

"Oh, nothing!" she blurted. "Just a slip of the tongue. Never mind." She glanced around, looking everywhere but at me. "Where is Sawyer, anyway? I thought for sure he'd be here."

I blushed again and shook my head, letting loose the sigh I'd been trying to hold in. "I don't know if he'll come." I'd texted Sawyer along with everyone else, but my phone had died before I'd gotten a response from him. I'd been hoping he would show, and I'd even put a sprig of mistletoe in my pocket just in case, thinking that if I had the chance, I might be able to make up for our botched kiss. But each time I glanced down the street, all I saw was an empty sidewalk. I shrugged. "I guess I'd understand if he didn't come. I mean, I know how he feels about the holidays. And he always stands by what he believes."

"It's three o' clock already," Nyssa said, frowning.

"Maybe he'll still turn up," I said. I laughed at Nyssa's disgruntled look, and then a thought struck me. "Hey, did *you* have anything to do with the Secret Santa gifts I got from Sawyer? He told me somebody helped him, and I thought maybe you—"

"No," Nyssa said, a little too quickly, dropping her eyes. "It wasn't me. Sorry." She looked oddly sheepish.

I felt a sudden rush of suspicion. "But you know who did, don't you?"

Her brow furrowed uncertainly and she glanced around, checking to see who might hear. "Maybe, but I can't tell you!" She smiled apologetically. "I *promised*!"

She did know! "Oh, come on, Nyssa," I pleaded. "You *love* gossip."

She bit her lip and nodded. "I do. I *really* do. But this person. Well, they're worried you wouldn't like knowing. That it would make things . . . awkward."

"What? What do you mean?"

At that moment, a bunch of kids brushed by us, chattering, and Nyssa clammed up. "Sorry. I'm going to help make some bows for the porch," she said, then hurried away before I could say another word.

I sighed in frustration, but decided to let it go for now, resolving to corner her after this was over and get an answer. I glanced around at the yard. Slowly, it was coming together. The lights were restrung across the front of the house, we'd salvaged most of the animals and arranged them in scenes in the yard.

Alex and I started building an igloo to take the place of Santa's workshop. Alex even had the great idea of sticking some of the lights inside of it, so that if the power came back on, color-changing lights would make the igloo glow from the inside out. We worked side by side, and we didn't say much, but I felt Alex's eyes studying me more than once. My heart sped up. Had he heard me and Nyssa talking? I was sure he wanted to say something about Sawyer, but each time I glanced his direction, he looked away, and the moment passed. Finally, we pushed the last block into place, and stood back to survey our work.

"It's even better than Santa's workshop," I said, and Alex grinned in agreement.

"We make a good team," he said quietly.

The igloo was big enough for at least two people to stand comfortably inside. We'd placed some of the penguins on the tiers of snow blocks, and made a sign to hang over the entrance that read: SANTA'S ICE PALACE. Around the edge of the igloo ran an electric train that glee-clubber Sam and his father had brought over. The light-up boxcars were all set to chug cheerily around the track once the electricity came on. *If* it came on.

There was a tap on my shoulder, and I turned to see Jez beside me, nibbling on one of the cookies Mom had made to fortify us as we worked.

"I think we're done," she said with a smile, and I nodded.

"Everything looks terrific," I said to our friends. "Thank you, guys, for all your help. Mom heated up some hot apple cider if you want to go inside for some while we wait. And hopefully, in about ten minutes, it'll be showtime!"

There were some claps and whoops from the kids scattered throughout the yard, and then Jez led them inside for cider.

I glanced up at the sky, which was already purpling into dusk. "I'm going to grab my camera and take some pictures of this for Dad," I said to Alex, "before I lose the light."

I went to my room for my camera. As I took it off my desk, my eyes fell on my elf costume from the mall, sitting in a pile in the corner. I smiled as an idea struck me, and in a moment of spontaneity or lunacy (I wasn't sure which), I reached for it.

When I came back outside, my heart stopped short at the sight of Sawyer standing in the yard with Alex. Both of them had their hands in their pockets and looked like they were straining for things to say.

"Hey," I said. They glanced up together, and I felt a wave of heat sweep my face. As their eyes focused on me, I had the sense that both of them seemed to be asking the same silent question, but I didn't have a clue what it was.

"What's with the elf getup?" Sawyer said, his head tilting in confusion.

"Oh, I . . ." My voice trailed off. "I—I'm getting in touch with my holiday spirit!"

Sawyer's brow crinkled in confusion. "I thought you hated Christmas."

I shrugged. "I had a change of heart," I said softly.

"Huh," he muttered, casting another long glance at my elf ears.

I waited to feel a shudder of embarrassment, but it never came. Instead, what I felt was the certainty of knowing that I'd have to tell him everything. The sooner the better. Alex had been right all along. The Emery that Sawyer had seen before had been trying so hard to be the sort of someone he'd fall for. Now it was time to let every side of myself show, and let him decide whether he liked all of me or not.

With pulse racing, I faced Sawyer. "I wasn't sure you got my text," I said.

"Yeah, I got it," he said. "I was in the groove with some music stuff earlier, and stringing lights and ornaments would kill my muse. Can't let that happen. Nothing comes before my music." He grinned. "I figured you'd get that."

"Oh. Uh-huh." I didn't get it, though. So many of my friends had dropped everything to help me today. But Sawyer couldn't find the time? My smile dimmed as my chest tightened in disappointment.

"Anyway," he continued, "I walked over to see if you still wanted to go to the movies. The theater over in Boonton has power backup, and my mom can drive us over—"

"I'm going to grab some cider," Alex mumbled, excusing himself to head for the house. "See you later, Sawyer."

I gave Alex a hesitant smile, trying to send him a silent "thanks" for giving Sawyer and me a minute alone. But he ducked his head and turned away.

I focused back on Sawyer. "Um. The movies. Right." I twisted my gloves in my hand, my pulse hammering in my throat. Yesterday, I would've jumped at the chance to escape the Holiday Stroll. Yesterday, I would never have felt this kind of anticipation over a bunch of people gawking at our house. But a lot had happened since yesterday. "What if we hung out here?" I suggested.

"At your house?" His enthusiasm dipped a notch, and he scanned the yard with a look of mild disinterest. "I don't get it. You told me you weren't into any of this."

"I know I did. But we just finished fixing up the Holly Jolly House, and any minute now the power might be coming back to our street." I sucked in a breath. "I want to stay here to see it light up. We've been working so hard . . ."

"We?" Sawyer repeated. "You and Alex?"

I nodded. "And everyone else, too. But Alex's been here since this morning. He's been great helping out."

"I believe it." Sawyer shook his head, giving a short laugh. "He's like an elf himself, that guy. Nice enough, but that 'ho-ho-ho' attitude gets on my nerves."

I stiffened, and before I had time to think, I found myself saying, "I love the way Alex looks at things. I mean, when he talks to little kids about Christmas, their faces light up. He's got this enthusiasm that's totally infectious. It's—it's"—I grinned, shrugging—"magic." Sawyer raised his eyebrows in surprise, but I gulped and kept going. "And if you think his attitude is so annoying, then what do you think about mine?"

Sawyer scoffed. "You're in some guilt phase with your dad, that's all. It'll pass." He leaned forward. "I know you, Em."

"I'm not sure you do," I said quietly. "I didn't think I *was* into Christmas. Not anymore. But I wasn't being honest with myself. And . . ." I bolstered myself for the next revelation. "I haven't been honest with you, either." I motioned to my elf costume. "This costume isn't just because of the Holly Jolly House. I've been wearing it for the last month, whenever I work at the North Pole Wonderland at the mall."

His brow creased in confusion. "You mean, the Santa photo booth?"

I nodded. "I've been working there with my parents, but I didn't want you to know. I was embarrassed, but now I see how stupid that was. I had the chance to give all these kids something special, and blew it." I sighed, clutching Grandma's locket for courage. "But . . . this costume, these decorations, this season. I love it. I always have. I had just—kind of tried to push it aside. To forget about it. Until someone reminded me."

Alex's face popped into my head, and my heart picked up its pace.

Sawyer stared down at the snow for a long minute. "Okay," he said slowly. "So, what is it you really want, Em?"

I smiled. "Tonight? I want to light up the Holly Jolly House with my dad. After that . . ." I shrugged, laughing lightly. "Well, I guess that's as far as I've gotten."

Sawyer nodded. "I could stay, but since we're being honest, I'd be lousy at handing out candy canes and giving good tidings, all that jazz." He smiled, and I was relieved to see understanding in his face. He seemed to realize in that moment, as I did, that he and I didn't have that much in common in the end.

I looked into those amber eyes that I'd dreamed about for so long and, for the first time, saw them without a crush-induced haze. When I did that, they didn't seem nearly as irresistible as they once had.

"Anyway, if you change your mind about the movies down the road, give me a call." Sawyer took a step toward the sidewalk and waved. "It's been fun, getting to know you better."

I recovered my senses long enough to give him a grateful smile. "You too." I waved. "See you later."

I turned toward the house, feeling lighter from knowing I'd done the right thing with Sawyer. As my foot touched the first porch step, there was a blinding flash, and in an instant, the Holly Jolly House was ablaze with thousands of colored lights and singing, dancing animals. Our power was back on!

The rest of the neighborhood was still dark, but the Holly Jolly House illuminated everything. My front door flew open and everyone ran down the steps, clapping and hollering and dancing around the glimmering yard.

Jez, Lyra, and Rafael grabbed baskets of candy canes to get ready for incoming holiday strollers. Nyssa gathered a group of glee kids along the porch to sing carols. Alex's *abuelo* carried a tray of hot cocoa to the edge of our driveway to pass out mugs to the crowd. The last ones out the door were Mom and Dad, who was leaning gingerly on Mom for support.

"Emery." Dad beamed, pulling me into a hug. "You did all this?"

"I had a lot of help," I said.

He shook his head. "I don't believe it." He glanced around, taking in the dancing animals and twinkling lights. The boyish grin he'd been missing the last week spread wide across his face.

"Do you think Grandma would've liked it?" I whispered, pressing my face into his chest.

"Oh, Em. She would've loved it."

I felt my heart lift, and then I turned as Jez tapped my shoulder.

"Guys," she said, "you've *got* to see this." She nodded toward the end of our street, where at least a hundred people were walking with flashlights, heading for our house. The Holiday Stroll was happening after all! Leading the parade was the Light & Power driver from this morning, holding hands with his two children.

He waved at me. "You kept your promise. I kept mine."

"How did you do it?" I asked.

He grinned. "Santa works his magic with flying reindeer, I work mine with a pair of pliers."

"Merry Christmas!" I cried, not caring if I sounded over-the-top jolly. Then I caught sight of Sophie, the little girl who I'd made cry the afternoon I told her I wasn't a real elf. She was standing in line with her mom.

I kneeled down in front of her while her mom looked on warily.

"Hey, Sophie," I said cheerfully. "Remember me? Emery Elf?"

She looked doubtful for a second, then hesitantly nodded.

I leaned toward her conspiratorially. "I wanted to tell you that your mom was right. I was undercover that day, protecting my identity. We have to disguise ourselves as ordinary humans every once in a while, for the top secret elf work we have to do. But I'm here to tell you firsthand, we're real. And so is Santa. Can I trust you to keep our secret?" I winked, and her mouth dropped open in awe as she nodded.

I gave her a thumbs-up, then handed her a candy cane. "I'm so glad Santa and I can count on you."

Sophie grinned at me, her eyes sparkling. I stood up to nod to her mom, who gave me a relieved smile. Then I scanned the yard again for Alex, wondering where he was in all the fray.

"Hey, have you seen Alex?" I asked Nyssa as the rest of the carolers warmed up. "I figured he'd be on the hot cocoa crusade with Señor Perez by now."

Her brow furrowed. "I thought you knew. He went home. While you were outside talking to Sawyer."

"What?" My heart sank. "But he didn't even say good-bye."

Nyssa shrugged. "I guess he figured you were too busy with Sawyer."

"Not even close," I said absently, disappointment overshadowing the happiness I'd felt only a minute ago. "It turns out I was wrong about Sawyer. He's not for me." Nyssa's jaw dropped, but I shook my head. "No, I'm good with it. I should've realized it before."

Nyssa tapped her finger against her chin thoughtfully. "I had you two pegged for happily-ever-after."

"I think I fell for the *idea* of Sawyer. The real deal was different." I searched the yard again. "I can't believe Alex just left," I murmured. "It doesn't seem right without him here. I just don't get why—"

"I think I do," Nyssa cut in. "I mean, he never fessed up to his feelings straight out, but it makes perfect sense . . ." Her voice trailed off as she stared at the ground, debating. Then she nodded like she'd made up her mind. "I have to tell you something, Em. He's going to kill me, but . . ." She clenched her eyes shut and blurted, "Remember the mystery person who helped Sawyer with your gifts? It was Alex." She clapped a hand over her mouth. "Thank goodness it's finally out! I wanted to tell you so many times, but he made me swear not to."

My stomach dropped to my toes as I stared at her, speechless. *What* had she just said? When I finally found my voice, I whispered, "You mean, Alex picked out my Secret Santa gifts?"

She nodded. "Every single one. I heard him talking about it with Sawyer in the hallway at school one day. Sawyer said that if Alex hadn't been helping him, he wouldn't have had a clue what to get you. Alex realized that I'd heard everything, but he made me promise not to tell you. I wondered why Alex would want to help, but when I saw the way he was looking at you earlier today, it was so obvious." She gripped my hands with her mittened ones. "He likes you, Em. I think he really likes you."

"I can't believe it." The ground underneath my feet seemed to be surging, and I was reeling with it, stunned by what I'd heard. All this time I'd been so convinced that Sawyer understood me so well, better than anyone. All this time, it had been *Alex* picking out the perfect gifts for me. Alex. Alex . . .

"I had to tell you," Nyssa went on, "because I think you might feel the same way?"

Realization struck, and I blushed crazily. "Oh. No," I started, flustered. "It's not like that . . ."

"Not yet," she said, "but did you ever think that maybe you want it to be?"

I opened my mouth to deny it, then found with astonishment that I couldn't. I smiled, in relief and excitement as the emotions that had seemed so muddled in my head swiftly snapped into place. Why had it taken me so long to see what was right in front of my face? I didn't know, but all I cared about now was putting everything to rights.

"I'm going to go find him," I declared to Nyssa, and she beamed.

I spun around and nearly slammed into Mom and Dad.

"I see our resident photographer's falling down on the job," Dad said teasingly.

Mom nodded. "How about a few pics for posterity?"

"Actually, there's something I really need to do," I started, but then caved when Dad's face fell. "Okay. One for now, and then I promise to take more in a bit."

I lifted my camera and snapped a picture of the Holly Jolly House in all its glittery glory. It was a truly inspiring sight. The most beautiful thing about it, though, wasn't the lights or the music, but the jubilant smiles on the faces of the dozens of people basking in its glow.

After I showed Mom and Dad the photo, I hurriedly put my camera back in its case. "I have to go find Alex. I need to talk to him."

Mom looked at me quizzically, then laughed. "Well, you don't need to search too hard. He's right behind you."

My heart sprang to my throat as I turned. There he was. Alex, grinning at me and holding two steaming cups in his hands.

"I—I thought you left," I stammered. "You didn't say good-bye. I thought . . ."

"Thought what?" he said, taking a step closer.

I took a deep breath. "I thought you left because of Sawyer."

He dropped his eyes to the ground. "I know that I can't do anything to change the way you feel about him. I didn't leave because of him."

"You didn't?" I asked doubtfully. He shook his head ada-mantly, but I wasn't buying it for a second. "Okay, well, if you're sure," I said, faking nonchalance even as my heart raced, "then I need you to come with me."

Before I lost my courage completely, I grabbed his arm and pulled him toward our igloo. We breezed by Nyssa, who was standing beside Jez, giving her a whispered earful. I could only guess it was a detailed lowdown on what was happening with Alex and me, because when Jez glanced my direction, she gave me a wide-eyed look, followed by an encouraging thumbs-up. I laughed. So much for Nyssa keeping secrets. I guessed it was only a matter of minutes before the entire Fairview student body knew what was going on, but I didn't care. The only thing I cared about was that Alex was right here, right now, hopefully still liking me.

"What are we doing in here?" he asked once we were inside the igloo. He set the cups on the ground and faced me, perplexed, his dark curls falling across his forehead. The soft red and green lights undulated against the snowy walls, casting colorful shadows across his face. Suddenly, I had a strong sense of déjà vu. This had happened before. But when? My heart stopped. In my dream! The dream where I'd been about to kiss Sawyer. Only the boy in my dream hadn't been Sawyer at all. He'd been Alex.

I smiled, taking a step closer to him. "I have a special delivery for you," I said, reaching into my pocket. "From *your* Secret Santa."

He blinked at me blankly. "Really? I didn't even know I had one."

Summoning every ounce of courage I had, I pulled the sprig of mistletoe out of my pocket and hung it over our heads.

Alex looked up, redness blooming furiously across his cheeks. "Um, what are you doing?"

I laughed over my pounding pulse. "Don't tell me Santa's biggest fan doesn't know what to do with mistletoe!"

"Oh, I know what to do," he bumbled. "I just wasn't sure you wanted—"

I didn't let him finish. I stood on my toes and kissed him. The kiss was breathtaking and sweet. Everything I'd always thought a first kiss should be. Everything that Sawyer's wasn't. I knew, with more certainty than ever before, that Alex was who I belonged with. It wasn't logical, or perfect. Alex made me feel off-balance and challenged. We'd probably end up fighting as much as we laughed, but that would only make it more exciting. My heart had known this all along. It had just taken my head a while to catch up.

I pulled away to see Alex smiling at me—a bigger smile than I'd ever seen on him before, and that was saying something.

I whispered into his ear, "It was you all along giving Sawyer the ideas for gifts."

He nodded. "I've had a crush on you since the first time I saw you at school. You didn't even know I existed, but I kept hoping. And when you started working at the mall, I finally got up the courage to talk to you." He pulled me closer. "I wanted to tell you how I felt, so many times. But I thought if I was ever going to have a real shot with you, you'd have to figure out everything on your own. And . . ." He grinned. "My theory about you was right."

I laid my head against his shoulder. "It's you who really gets me. I'm sorry I didn't see it before."

He brushed my hair out of my eyes. "And *I'm* sorry I didn't get to give you any of the gifts in person. But now I do." He reached for the steaming cups on the ground and handed me one brimming with marshmallows. "Merry Christmas."

"Thanks," I said, feeling a touch of confusion, "but . . . you know I don't like hot chocolate."

He shook his head. "*This* is what I went home for. I think I finally made some hot cocoa you will like." He nodded toward the cup. "Go ahead. Try it."

I took a tentative sip, then another, longer one. I closed my eyes. The hot chocolate wasn't like any I'd ever tasted before. It was bittersweet and rich, with an unexpected bite. It was the perfect combination of sweet and spicy. "Yum." I sipped again. "I love it."

"Victory is mine at last!" Alex cried, hugging me while I laughed. "I figured out what was missing. I added in some crushed Oaxacan chilies. Ordinary hot chocolate would never do for a girl as extraordinary as you." He grinned as I blushed. "Abuelo says we'll start selling it in the store next week."

"But it needs a name," I said. "What are you going to call it?"

"I have the perfect name for it." He leaned close and gave me another sweet, lingering kiss. "Hot Cocoa Kiss. Of course."

hot
cocoa
recipes

There is nothing cozier than cuddling up with a cup of hot cocoa on a cold winter's day! With the perfect recipes, Alex finally convinced Emery to give in to her cocoa cravings, and now you can enjoy them, too! Just remember to always have adult supervision when you're using a stovetop or oven, or when you're handling hot foods.

These toasty treats will be sure to melt your heart!

Caramel Crush

4 cups whole milk

1/2 cup sugar

1/4 cup unsweetened cocoa powder (for Oaxacan hot
    chocolate, use 5 discs of Mexican chocolate, which can be
    found online or at your local grocery store)

3/4 tsp vanilla extract

1/4 cup caramel sauce (can be found with ice-cream
    toppings in your local grocery store)

Whipped cream

Dash of coarse sea salt

On the stove, heat milk, sugar, and cocoa powder or chocolate discs in a medium saucepan until just boiling. Remove from heat and add vanilla and most of the caramel sauce, then stir. With an adult helping you, carefully pour into mugs. Garnish with whipped cream, drizzle with remaining caramel sauce, and sprinkle with a dash of sea salt. Makes six servings. Enjoy!

Cinna-more

4 cups whole milk
1/2 cup sugar
1 tsp cinnamon
1/4 cup unsweetened cocoa powder (for Oaxacan hot
    chocolate, use 5 discs of Mexican chocolate, which can be
    found online or at your local grocery store)
3/4 tsp vanilla extract
Whipped cream
Miniature marshmallows
Chocolate shavings

On the stove, heat milk, sugar, cinnamon, and cocoa powder or
chocolate discs in a medium saucepan until just boiling. Remove
from heat and add vanilla, then stir. With an adult helping you,
carefully pour into mugs. Garnish with whipped cream and
marshmallows, and sprinkle with cinnamon and chocolate
shavings. Makes six servings. Enjoy!

Hot Cocoa Kiss

4 cups whole milk
3 tbsp brown sugar
1/8 tsp cinnamon
1/8 tsp Pasilla de Oaxaca chili powder (can be found online
    or in specialty spice stores. Or use 1/8 tsp basic chili
    powder instead)
1/4 cup unsweetened cocoa powder (for Oaxacan hot
    chocolate, use 5 discs of Mexican chocolate, which can be
    found online or at your local grocery store)
3/4 tsp vanilla extract
Whipped cream
Miniature marshmallows

On the stove, heat milk, sugar, cinnamon, Pasilla de Oaxaca powder, and cocoa powder or chocolate discs in a medium saucepan until just boiling. Remove from heat and add vanilla, then stir. With an adult helping you, carefully pour into mugs. Garnish with whipped cream and marshmallows, and sprinkle with a dash of cinnamon and chili powder. Makes six servings. Enjoy!

MORE DELICIOUS TREATS FROM SUZANNE NELSON!

bake
pop
crush

suzanne nelson

wish

SCHOLASTIC

Alicia Ramirez has always loved baking. But Ali's sweet life turns sour when a sleek coffee shop opens across the street, giving her family's bakery a run for its money. Worst of all, the owner's son, Dane McGuire, likes to bake, too… and happens to be annoyingly cute.

When Lise Santos stumbles into a bakery's midnight taste test, she meets a supercute boy. He's as sweet as the macarons they share, and Lise is totally smitten. But when she discovers who her mystery guy is, he's not at all what she expected. Is this a recipe for total disaster?

macarons at midnight

wish

SCHOLASTIC

What's on your  list?

13 Gifts
WENDY MASS

The Last Present
WENDY MASS

TWICE UPON A TIME
Beauty and the Beast
The Only One Who Didn't Run Away.
WENDY MASS

Switched at Birthday
Natalie Standiford

Once Upon a Cruise

Playing Cupid

hot cocoa hearts

you're bacon me crazy

SCHOLASTIC
scholastic.com/wish
SCHOLASTIC and associated logos are trademarks and/or registered trademarks of Scholastic Inc.

WISH2